NO PLACE FOR MARRIAGE

(MURDER IN THE KEYS: BOOK #4)

JADEN SKYE

Books by Jaden Skye

THE CARIBBEAN MURDER SERIES
DEATH BY HONEYMOON (Book #1)
DEATH BY DIVORCE (Book #2)
DEATH BY MARRIAGE (Book #3)
DEATH BY DESIRE (Book #4)
DEATH BY DECEIT (Book #5)
DEATH BY JEALOUSY (Book #6)
DEATH BY PROPOSAL (Book #7)
DEATH BY OBSESSION (Book #8)
DEATH BY DEVOTION (Book #9)
DEATH BY BETRAYAL (Book #10)
DEATH BY REQUEST (Book #11)
DEATH BY ENGAGEMENT (Book #12)
DEATH BY SEDUCTION (Book #13)
DEATH BY TEMPTATION (Book #14)
DEATH BY INVITATION (Book #15)
DEATH BY WEDDING (Book #16)

THE TOM'S RIVER SAGA
A PERFECT STRANGER (Book #1)

MURDER IN THE KEYS
NO PLACE TO DIE (Book #1)
NO PLACE TO VANISH (Book #2)
NO PLACE FOR VENGEANCE (Book #3)
NO PLACE FOR MARRIAGE (Book #4)

THE KILLING GAME
INVITATION TO DIE (Book #1)
INVITATION TO MADNESS (Book #2)
INVITATION TO AGONY (Book #3)

ISBN: 978-1-64029-214-7

CHAPTER ONE

When Bella finally pushed open the sliding glass doors and stepped out onto the deck of Tyron's gorgeous beach house, it was hard to breathe. A fog had rolled in from the ocean and the air had grown stultifying all over Naples. As she did so many other evenings, she had to check when Tyron wanted his dinner. Working as an aide for Tyron for so many years had its up and downs—fortunately, things had at least remained stable. But change was happening. In the past few months Tyron had definitely been going downhill, though no one in the family dared to say a word about it.

It was later than usual and Bella hadn't seen Tyron's stunning twenty-nine-year-old wife, Megan, all day. Megan was probably still upstairs in her quarters or out shopping, spending Tyron's fortune as fast as she possibly could. God forbid Megan should take a tray out to him.

Now it was past Tyron's dinner time, and Bella felt uneasy. Usually he rang the bell, or called for her to bring his dinner out onto the back patio. He loved eating there, sitting in his wheelchair, overlooking the ocean and sand.

But today he hadn't called.

He probably fell asleep on the deck, thought Bella.

But Bella was surprised, as she'd walked outside, that Tyron hadn't said anything to her. Usually he greeted her with some comment or other.

She looked around for him and to her total amazement, the wheelchair was there, near the top of the stairs. But it was empty! What was going on?

Shocked, Bella spun around, her eyes frantically darting. It made no sense. Tyron was bound to his wheelchair; there was no way he could have gotten out of it by himself. Was it possible he could have somehow fallen out of it and, using his arms, crawled over to a far corner that she couldn't see in the fog?

"Tyron," Bella yelled into the thick air. "Where are you? Answer me!"

A heavy silence greeted her.

"Tyron, where are you?" Bella's voice rose excitedly, as she flew around the edge of the patio, looking for him.

Suddenly, Bella stopped racing.

She glanced down onto the beach and froze.

A horrible sight met her eyes. Tyron was sprawled out on the sand, face down.

"Tyron!" Bella screamed, racing down the wooden steps to where he lay. "Tyron, answer me!"

Immediately, she felt for a pulse. It wasn't there.

"Tyron, Tyron." Bella pounded his chest and shook his inert body. No response.

She put her mouth on his to breathe life back into him.

Nothing. He was cold.

Bella took a step back and stared unbelievingly. Tyron's scratched face was covered with sand. How did this happen? How long had he been here?

Bella knew she had to call the police immediately. But what would she say? She was the one here with him all day and the one who'd found him.

Bella's thoughts flew in a thousand directions. Was this a horrible accident? Had Tyron fallen out of his wheelchair and down the steps?

Or had someone pushed him?

Bella trembled uncontrollably as she stayed beside him on the sand. Tyron was her responsibility and he'd ended up dead. She was terrified to imagine who did it and what would happen next.

There was no choice, she realized, but to climb the stairs back up to the patio.

It was time to call for help.

CHAPTER TWO

Olivia smiled as she looked at the plaque on the door. The name had been changed from "Olivia Wells, Private Investigator" to "Wells and Darrington Investigations." It felt wonderful to have a partner to build the company with.

Olivia and Wayne were almost finished settling into their office in Key West, and Olivia looked over at Wayne, in the midst of hanging a painting on the wall over his desk. A screen had been placed between Wayne's desk and hers, delineating their work spaces. They would work together, but also have their own roles and specialties. It was empowering to create a company for those who wanted both a male and a female point of view on a case.

"I'm almost finished." Wayne grinned over his shoulder at Olivia.

"Looks great," she replied.

It felt natural to be working with Wayne, almost inevitable, actually. When Olivia and Wayne placed an announcement in the papers about their new partnership, calls came in one after another. Many congratulated them and quite a few mentioned the article about them that had recently been published in the *South Florida Chronicle*. Word was getting out, and it was exciting.

"Now we just have to get the call for our first case." Wayne laughed.

Olivia felt certain that the call would be coming any moment. It felt like it was just around the corner.

"How about us grabbing a quick dinner when we're finished here?" Olivia replied lightly. It was easy and casual, having meals together now; the tension had gone out of it. It was just part of their daily routine.

"Great idea," Wayne answered as he stood back examining his handiwork. The painting he'd just hung was of hunters in the woods looking for wild game. Wayne's father and brother had been hunters and bequeathed the painting to him. He put it up there now to honor them.

"The painting looks good," said Olivia.

"Yes, it does," Wayne agreed as he turned toward her. "Okay, enough in here for now, let's go out before it gets dark."

Wayne knew that Olivia enjoyed being outdoors at twilight, before the streets and restaurants became crowded. He was aware that she liked feeling that she still had part of the day to enjoy before the evening. Olivia appreciated that Wayne thought of that now. It didn't surprise her, though. There were all kinds of ways in which he was sensitive and caring.

As they turned to the door to leave, the phone suddenly started ringing. They glanced at it briefly and then at one another. Without a word, Olivia quickly picked up.

"Wells and Darrington Investigations?" a woman's frantic voice sounded on the other end.

"Yes?" asked Olivia.

"Is this Olivia Wells herself?" The woman's voice rose noticeably.

"Yes, it is," said Olivia, "how can I help you?"

"This is Megan Barr," the distressed woman breathed on the other end. "I'm calling you from the police station in Naples. I read all about you and your company. I was very impressed."

"Thank you," said Olivia. "How can we be of help?"

Megan paused for a long moment on the other end of the phone. "My husband has come to harm," she finally managed to utter.

"Harm?" Olivia wondered if he was still alive. "What do you mean exactly?"

"I mean Tyron's gone," breathed Megan.

"Did this happen recently?" asked Olivia.

"I'm Tyron Barr's wife," the woman announced fitfully, as if Olivia should certainly know who he was. "Tyron's well known. He's rich, he's famous." Megan paused and waited for a response.

Olivia hadn't heard of her husband, however. "Tell me more," she replied.

"Tyron was found dead on the beach at our home in Naples," Megan continued, her words pouring out fast now. "He was wheelchair bound and his aide found him a few hours ago."

"A few hours ago? I'm very sorry," breathed Olivia.

Megan didn't seem to hear a word Olivia said. "Tyron was laying at the bottom of a staircase leading from the patio down onto the beach," she continued, fitfully. "Bella didn't know I was home at the time. She took it upon herself to call the police immediately. The police are at our house now, scanning everything, searching for evidence of any kind."

"Where were you when this happened?" asked Olivia. It was all very recent and shocking and Olivia felt her heart beat faster.

"I was upstairs in my home office and didn't hear a thing," Megan exclaimed. "Bella and I were the only ones at home when the incident took place."

The incident? It was an odd way for a wife to put it, thought Olivia. Way too impersonal. "Where are you now, Megan?"

"I told you I'm at the police station." Megan's voice cracked.

Olivia was startled. "Already?" It seemed very fast. "How come?"

"After they took Tyron's body to the medical examiner, the police brought Bella and I into the station for questioning." Megan's voice grew brittle. "They said it was just routine."

"That's rough," breathed Olivia.

"You can say that again! It's rough and it's crazy and I need help." Megan suddenly broke into tears. "I told them I wouldn't say another thing without my lawyer. And, I want my own private investigator too!"

"I can certainly understand that," Olivia murmured.

"Can you come down to Naples right away?" Megan pleaded.

"I actually think it's possible," Olivia replied. "I'll have to check with my partner."

"Please, please, I need you here with me." Megan was beside herself.

"I don't see why we can't," Olivia continued. "Let me talk to him."

"I need you," Megan rallied. "No one here believes a word I say."

"Why don't they?" Olivia felt concerned.

"I'm much, much younger than Tyron. So, naturally the cops are suspicious of me," Megan breathed. "Everyone's always had something to say about our age difference! When will you let me definitely know if you can come?" Megan kept up the pressure.

Megan sounded as sharp and calculating as could be; not exactly like a grieving widow.

"Let me talk to my partner now and call you right back," Olivia replied.

"Okay, make it fast. I'll be sitting at the phone," Megan responded. "I have plenty of resources and I'll pay you well. I've got to have my name cleared immediately."

Olivia took Megan's number and hung up the phone.

"Who was that?" Wayne asked, fascinated.

"It's a young woman, Megan Barr," Olivia exclaimed. "Her husband, Tyron, an older man, was just found dead on the beach at their house in Naples."

"Tyron Barr?" Wayne's eyes opened. "I've heard of him. He's a rich tycoon who throws huge parties. He's in the papers a lot."

"What kind of parties? What's he famous for?" Olivia was surprised.

"Who said he's famous?" asked Wayne.

"Megan just mentioned that Tyron was well known."

"He's well known but not famous," Wayne replied. "Tyron's in the papers because of his events, many of which are for charitable foundations. He's wheelchair bound, isn't he?"

Olivia was impressed with how much Wayne knew about him. "Yes, he is," she responded. "Megan was at the police station when she called. Seems like they took her and his aide in for questioning right away."

Wayne grimaced. "The police took her in immediately?"

"They told her it was just routine. She and the aide were the only two at the home when it happened," said Olivia. "And she said no one there seems to believe her."

Wayne shook his head slowly. "Why not?"

"She's much younger than he is," Olivia replied. "I suppose that might look suspicious."

"Might?" Wayne looked away. "This doesn't look good for her, does it?"

"No, it doesn't, of course," Olivia agreed. "Megan wants her name cleared immediately and she also wants us to help find the killer."

Wayne took a quick breath. "This could definitely be a trap for us," he said. "It would be smart of her to use us as foils. Hiring detectives to find the killer could definitely take suspicion off her for a while."

"It could," said Olivia. "But that would backfire if she's guilty anyway, wouldn't it?"

"Maybe, maybe not," Wayne responded. "Who knows what she has in mind? Unfortunately, cases like this are often open and shut. Especially if the only ones on the premises were the young wife and the old husband's aide."

"Really? Open and shut?" Olivia was surprised.

"Sure," Wayne continued, "Florida's well known for the black widows that drift down this way. I hope Megan doesn't want us digging up false evidence to cover for her."

"Black widows?" Olivia asked.

"Young women who marry rich, old guys and spend their money like it was water," said Wayne. "In Florida, when a marriage ends, each partner gets half, fifty-fifty. Sooner or later these marriages end and the wives end up with a bundle. Most of the marriages end by divorce, but often things go a little further. These husbands can turn up dead for all kinds of strange reasons."

"That's why the police don't believe her?" asked Olivia.

"Probably," Wayne conceded. "And that's probably why they took her in for questioning so fast."

"All the more reason we should take the case," Olivia retorted. "To get to the truth of the matter!"

Wayne looked glum, however. "Perhaps," he said.

"You don't look happy about it." Olivia pressed him.

"Of course I'm happy to have a case," he answered. "It's just not exactly the kind I thought we'd begin with."

"You never know what it will turn into," Olivia murmured. "There's always much more to it than meets the eye. True?"

"Yes, of course it's true. We have no idea what lays up ahead," Wayne agreed. "Okay. I'm in. Key West is only an hour flight to Naples. We'll be there and meet her at the police station in no time at all."

CHAPTER THREE

Olivia was excited to be sitting at the airport with Wayne, about to board the flight to Naples. Fortunately, the flights ran frequently and they were easily booked on the next one out. As they sat in the boarding area, she looked out at the evening sky. It seemed as if changes in her life came suddenly these days. Everything turned around in a moment, like tonight. She and Wayne were headed to have dinner and the next thing Olivia knew she was booked on a flight to Naples, to work on a new case.

"Beautiful night, isn't it?" Wayne commented as they gazed out of the windows at the vast sky spread before them. If you looked closely, you could even see the crescent of a new moon.

"Yes, it's a really beautiful night," said Olivia, wondering what it would be like when they landed. What was waiting for them up ahead?

"It'll be an easy flight," Wayne commented.

Olivia smiled. "It's not the flight I'm concerned about," she answered, "it's what happens after we arrive."

*

As Wayne had said, the flight was quick and easy and they landed and got to the Naples police station in what seemed like no time at all. The station was located in a long, sprawling, low building at the east side of town. As the taxi drove along the main avenue, lights were on in the upscale restaurants and shops. Well-dressed people everywhere were milling around, out and about, enjoying an evening of elegance and pleasure.

"Quite a high-end town," Olivia commented, as Wayne smiled.

"Naples is known for its expensive shops, restaurants, golf courses, and white sand beaches," he replied. "It's also full of parks, nature preserves, museums, shows, the works. Not exactly what you would expect for a town on the Gulf of Mexico."

"A place for the wealthy," Olivia noted.

"And for the unnecessarily pampered, perhaps." Wayne smiled.

Olivia wondered what he meant. Wayne had many sides to him and his offhand comments often took her aback. She realized that she would get to know him better as they worked together. She really looked forward to that.

The taxi arrived at the station and they got out quickly and made their way inside. Wayne had called ahead and let the police know that he and Olivia were on the way. There hadn't been any blowback about that. Fortunately, Wayne had a fine reputation and was well known in South Florida from his years on the police force in Key West.

The moment Olivia and Wayne walked through the front door, a young police officer approached them.

"Wells and Darrington Investigations," Wayne said as the officer held out his hand.

"Marcus Brandt here," the cop offered. "We're expecting you. Megan's with Chief of Police James Gallant in the back room now. She keeps telling us you two are coming and we haven't had much luck in talking to her. She's also lawyered up quickly, so there's not much more we can do."

"Who's her lawyer?" asked Wayne as they walked down the hallway with Marcus toward the room Megan was waiting in.

"Cameron Fern, heard of her?" Marcus threw Wayne a quick glance.

"Not really," said Wayne.

"She's as tough as they get," Marcus responded. "Cameron's well known in these parts for getting huge settlements for divorce clients. I didn't know she took on criminal cases as well."

"Has this been declared a criminal case already?" Olivia was surprised.

Marcus smiled at Olivia. "No, of course not yet," he conceded. "Not until the medical examiner's report comes in. But the handwriting's on the wall. There's a reason Megan chose someone like Cameron to represent her, got her own private investigators, to boot."

Olivia was surprised they'd jumped to that conclusion so quickly.

Wayne said nothing, just looked down at the floor as they continued to the interrogation room.

When they got there and walked in a woman was standing with her back to the door. The moment they entered, however, she spun around.

"Olivia and Wayne?" Megan looked enormously relieved. "Megan Barr here."

Olivia was fascinated to see her face to face. Megan was a startlingly beautiful, willowy, young woman, with long, dark chestnut hair and huge green eyes.

"Thank God you got here tonight," Megan spoke directly to Olivia.

It was disconcerting for Olivia to realize that Megan was about the same age as her and had been married for a while already. During the flight, Olivia and Wayne had gone over information available on Megan and Tyron. Olivia had learned that Tyron was now seventy years old. Megan had married him when she was twenty-three. They'd actually been together for almost seven years by now. Why in the world would Megan do that? She was beautiful, could have had anyone she wanted.

Now Megan stood here looking at Olivia with a desperate look in her eyes. "I'd like to talk to my Investigators privately," she said authoritatively to another officer in the room.

"Certainly," a tall, hefty officer responded. First he turned to Olivia and Wayne. "I'm James Gallant," he introduced himself. "Chief of Police in Naples."

Wayne took his hand and shook it. "Pleased to meet you," he said.

Chief Gallant nodded as he reached out to shake Olivia's hand next.

"Olivia Wells," she introduced herself as well.

"We've heard about your work," Gallant said to Olivia, "and of course, also the fine work of your partner, Wayne."

Olivia smiled, impressed by Gallant's courteous behavior.

"Megan couldn't have chosen a finer team," he went on. "We'll be delighted to have you working along with us."

"They're my investigators," Megan burst in. "I didn't hire them to assist you."

Chief Gallant turned toward Megan slowly. "All of law enforcement work together," he replied. "We're all after the same thing, aren't we? The truth."

Megan grimaced. "I need privacy," she repeated. "I'd like to talk to my investigators alone now."

Chief Gallant nodded once again at Olivia and Wayne before motioning to the other officers there. Then they all left the room.

Once Gallant was out of the room, Megan practically fell down onto a chair, running her hands through her hair feverishly.

"It's exhausting, he's exhausting," she muttered. "This day has been a total nightmare and they've made it much worse."

"I'm sorry about that." Olivia took a few steps toward her.

Megan looked up at Olivia. "I can see in everyone's eyes that they're blaming me. Except maybe you?"

"Nobody can blame you yet, they don't know what happened," Wayne chimed in. "They're just concerned."

"Well, I'm concerned too," Megan shot back. "But I don't trust a single cop here. Not a single one of them. They're all the same. They rush to judgment. Want to close things up fast."

"That's why you called us in on the case," Olivia responded.

"Absolutely." Megan's eyes flashed.

"And why you've already hired a lawyer," Wayne added.

"How do you know that?" Megan didn't like it. "One of the cops told you? You're in cahoots with them?"

"I'm not in cahoots with anyone," Wayne calmly answered. "And yes, one of the police officers did mention it when we arrived. It's public knowledge anyway."

"Everything's public knowledge when you're famous." Megan seemed to be at the end of her rope. "I need all the protection I can get. And of course I don't know what happened yet either. But one thing I do know is that they're going to dream all kinds of things up. How is it possible that Tyron just fell down the stairs by himself? He didn't, he couldn't get out of his wheelchair alone. Could not."

"Could he have tried this time?" asked Olivia.

"No, impossible, he could not have done it." Megan was positive. "One thing about Tyron, he was not stupid. He was many other things for sure, but stupid, no!"

"Was he sick? Could he have gotten dizzy, leaned over and fell?" asked Wayne.

"No, ridiculous," said Megan. "He wasn't sick. He sat out in the sun all the time. If he needed anything he rang the bell for Bella and she came immediately and looked after it. He wouldn't have risked his life in any way at all. Tyron intended to live forever." Megan's words had a rough edge about them as she rambled on.

"This must be terribly hard for you." Olivia tried to slow her down. "It must be a huge shock."

"It is terribly hard," Megan spit back, "but no, it's not a huge shock. In fact, I'm not surprised at all. In fact, I expected him to die."

Wayne looked amazed. "Not surprised? You expected your husband to die? Was it because of his illness?" On the plane Wayne and Olivia had quickly researched Tyron's condition on their computers. It was a neurological condition of unknown origins that often attacked the elderly. Tyron had had it now for about three years.

Megan shrugged. “I didn’t expect Tyron to die because of his illness,” she replied. “Tyron became sick about four years into our marriage. It’s a condition that often comes with age. It gets worse in phases. The first year Tyron could walk easily. Now he’s totally wheelchair bound.”

“That must have made life so much more difficult for you,” said Olivia, wondering how Megan coped with it.

Megan said nothing, just stared straight ahead.

“You’ve had Tyron thoroughly checked, of course?” Olivia pushed her.

“Checked? That’s putting it mildly,” Megan shot back. “Tyron has been to all the top neurologists. There was nothing we could do.”

“It’s a waiting game, isn’t it?” said Wayne, quietly. “Is that why you expected him to die?”

“Not to die, but to be killed,” Megan whispered, suddenly beside herself. “And I expected I’d be the one that everyone would point to.”

“Why?” Olivia felt alarmed.

“Because I’m the young, rich widow and it doesn’t look good.” Megan sneered. “But I was good to him all these years. I gave him what he wanted. And I married him when I was just a child.”

Olivia suddenly felt a huge wave of sadness for Megan. “Why?” she asked.

“Why not?” asked Megan bitterly. “It happens all the time. Young people fall in love with older people. They each give the other something they need.”

Wayne looked incredulous. “Are you saying you fell in love with Tyron?”

Megan seemed put off. “Yes, I did,” she declared. “Tyron dazzled me from the first second we met. Then after that night, he pursued me relentlessly. He knew what he wanted and always got it. That’s Tyron in a nutshell for you.”

“He didn’t want to die, though?” Olivia had to be sure.

“Of course he didn’t, I just told you that,” said Megan. “Are you suggesting he threw himself down on the sand? Ridiculous! Impossible!”

Olivia found Megan’s heated reaction fascinating. She knew her husband well, for sure. And she seemed to still care deeply about him.

Wayne took another tack though. He returned to Megan’s earlier comment. “Just tell me, please, how long two people can stay dazzled by each other when there's such a big age difference? How long can something like this last?"

"A long time," Megan responded fitfully. "Or as long as is necessary. Why measure relationships in days and years?"

Olivia found Megan's comment fascinating. Megan had been in her early twenties and Tyron in his sixties when they'd gotten together. It was definitely possible that Megan was yearning for a father, and Tyron was longing to be young again. They did give each other something they needed then. It made sense.

"Of course it's natural that everyone will turn against me now," Megan repeated. "I'm no fool. I see what people are thinking. But there are lots of other people around who could have wanted to harm Tyron."

"Who?" Wayne was all over it. "And why?"

Megan backed up a minute and stared right in Wayne's eyes. "Well, for starters, how about his aide, Bella? She was there when he died, wasn't she? She was the one who found him!"

"Yes, she was," said Olivia. "The police have talked to her too, haven't they?"

"They have," Megan replied. "But I doubt that they know how much Bella hated Tyron, really. I saw the rage flash across her face more and more as time went by. Deep down it seemed to me as if she were trapped and couldn't wait to get away from us all."

"What kept her there?" Wayne asked crisply.

"Bella hung on because she needed the money. She has a sick aunt she helps out. There were always big perks attached to working for Tyron and I'm sure he made it worth her time. But Bella was the one in charge when he died. She was the one in the house with him."

"So were you!" Wayne reminded her.

"But I wasn't nearby. I was upstairs working in my home office," Megan snapped.

"What do you do, Megan?" Olivia asked.

"I arrange networking parties," Megan replied. "It's my own personal business and I love what I do. I'm good at it."

"I'm sure you are," Olivia replied.

Bolstered by Olivia's comment, Megan plunged on. "There are other people who could have benefitted from Tyron's death, too. Tyron has two daughters, Kayle and Lana. They're about my age and have always hated me. My relationship with their father is a nightmare for them. They're totally jealous in every way. And, of course, when their father married me, a big portion of their inheritance went to me. If I'm found guilty of getting rid of Tyron, the girls will get their inheritance back, won't they?"

Megan would make a great detective, thought Olivia. She had every angle covered.

"Are you accusing Tyron's daughters of being complicit in their father's death?" Wayne seemed disturbed by the idea.

"I'm not accusing them, I'm suggesting it," Megan spit out. "I often wondered if something like this could happen. Now it's your job to find out. Did the daughters team up with Bella to do it? Or did they possibly hire someone else? During the afternoon while I was working I actually thought I heard voices in the house. I even wondered if someone was visiting."

"Did you go down to check?" Olivia asked.

"No, why should I? I had my life and Tyron had his. Sometimes he had visitors. It was no business of mine."

"Did you ask Bella if someone had been visiting?" Olivia pressed on.

"I did and she said no one was there," Megan replied. "Of course, when we were taken in by the police, we were both whisked into separate rooms. We didn't get much of a chance to talk to each other. I heard the police have let her go by now."

"And how about you?" asked Olivia. "When are they going to let you go?"

"I'm sure they're waiting for me to talk to you first," Megan replied. "They'll let me go after we talk, won't they?"

"Of course they will," said Olivia quickly. "There's no grounds to hold you here."

"Not for now, anyway," Wayne responded.

Megan turned to Wayne. "What do you mean not for now? What are you implying?"

"These things take time," Wayne responded quietly.

"Of course they take time, but what do you mean?" Megan faced Wayne staunchly.

"It all depends on what turns up," Wayne replied. "What I actually mean is that we've a long road ahead of us."

"And I intend to be part of it," Megan declared. "Stay in close touch and report to me regularly. I'll send you names of people to talk to. But please, start with Bella first."

Exhausted, Megan suddenly had little else to say. As things died down, Wayne put a call in to Chief Gallant, who promptly came back inside. He assured everyone present that after he spoke with Olivia and Wayne privately, he would spend a little more time with Megan. After that she could go.

"Is there someone to go back home with you?" asked Olivia, concerned.

"I'll call my best friend, Nellie." Megan suddenly whimpered. "She's the only one I want with me now."

CHAPTER FOUR

Olivia and Wayne then joined Chief Gallant in his small, wooden office down the hall. As soon as they were all seated, Chief Gallant smiled at Wayne.

"How can we be of help to you on the case?" he asked. "I'm happy to share what we have, and of course I know you will do the same."

Wayne looked at him carefully. "You can be certain we'll share as much as we can," he assured him.

"Good," said Gallant. "That works."

"To start, fill us in on whatever you have this far." Wayne seemed grateful for the cooperation.

"Of course, as you well know by now, we took both Megan and Bella in for preliminary questioning," Gallant said, "because they were both present at the scene of the crime. Routine."

"I realize," Wayne murmured.

"We've let Bella go and naturally will release Megan shortly as well. It's definitely too soon to hold her," Gallant continued.

"Too soon?" Olivia was put off by his comment.

"Of course," Gallant replied. "So far what we have points to her, of course, though the hard evidence is not yet in."

"What exactly points to Megan?" Olivia was piqued. It seemed extremely early to come to that conclusion.

Both Wayne and Gallant looked at Olivia oddly. "May-December relationships!" Gallant sighed. "We see them over and over down here. They rarely end well."

Olivia was offended. "You only see the ones that end badly, not the ones that do well."

"I can't dispute that." Gallant smiled slowly. "But when they do end badly, there's a pattern to them."

Olivia realized that was true, but there still seemed so much more at work here. "For all we know, at this point Tyron's death could have simply been an accident," she remarked. "He could have become stir crazy, pushed himself out of the chair, and stumbled."

"Anything is possible," Gallant agreed. "Someone even suggested he could have had a mini-stroke and not realized what he was doing. But it's for the medical examiner to decide. He's going to look carefully at the exact position of Tyron's body when he was found. And also anything that might be found in his body."

Olivia flinched. Was Gallant suggesting that Tyron had been poisoned? Was that why he felt suspicious of Megan? Naturally, she had total access to her husband all the time.

"The other alternative," Olivia mused out loud, "is that someone came from behind and pushed him out of the wheelchair."

"That's the more likely scenario," Gallant concurred.

"Tyron's well known in the area, did he have any enemies that you know of?" Olivia continued.

"That's what law enforcement is exploring right now as we speak," said Gallant. "He also had complicated business dealings. Tyron made his original money in steel and now funds a lot of organizations. Some are questionable, for sure. We're getting a forensic accountant to go over everything. Lots of high-profile people could be involved."

"Good," said Wayne, pleased by the suggestion.

"But the first consideration always goes to the people who were with him when he died. Right now there are only two that we know of," Gallant continued.

"Only one, really," Olivia murmured. "Bella was the one with him at the time."

"Actually, Bella seems much more upset by Tyron's death than Megan," Gallant interrupted. "Did you guys notice how cool and calculating Megan is? She has her eye on every little detail and I haven't heard her once say a word about her deceased husband."

"Everyone grieves differently," Olivia had to say. "Megan hasn't even had time to realize that Tyron's gone."

"It's interesting that you're on Megan's side," Wayne couldn't help remark. "I found her to be unsettling as well."

"I'm not on anyone's side," Olivia answered forthrightly. "But I'm not against anyone either."

"The question isn't for or against," Gallant interrupted, "it's exactly how did Tyron fall? Once we know that, we'll have a direction to go in. We also have to carefully review security footage both inside and outside of the house to see if there were any other visitors. Megan claims she heard people downstairs talking. She can't prove it, of course."

"She was upstairs in her office the entire time, wasn't she?" asked Olivia.

"That's right," said Gallant. "She claims she was working up there. When she finally went downstairs her husband had been dead for quite a while."

Wayne stood up hastily. "Let's stick with the facts as we get them," he said. "Speculation is always counterproductive at this point. The security footage will tell us a great deal."

Gallant seemed pleased by Wayne's comment. "Yes, it will," he added. "And of course, if there were other visitors, we're into a whole new ballgame, for sure. If not, we put a laser focus on the two women who were at the residence when he died."

"Right," agreed Wayne.

"What's your next move?" Gallant asked. "How can we help you both out?"

"Next step is for us to talk to Bella," said Wayne. "We heard you let her go."

"Yes, we did," said Gallant. "Bella spends six days a week at Tyron's home and on her day off goes to a small apartment she shares with an elderly older aunt about thirty miles away."

"Where is Bella now?" asked Olivia quickly.

"She left the station under the condition that she would remain at Tyron's home until we've made more headway in the investigation," Gallant reported.

"She had no objections to that?" Wayne checked.

"None at all," said Gallant promptly. "We found Bella to be very cooperative and tremendously upset. She said she would never leave at this time, anyway. She wants to stay close by for the funeral and also to help everyone out."

"Nice," said Wayne.

"Loyal," remarked Olivia.

"We found no reason to doubt her," Gallant added. "Go talk to her yourself first thing in the morning and see."

"That's exactly what we'll do," Olivia assured him.

*

Olivia and Wayne left the station tired but also filled with nervous energy. The hotel Wayne had booked for them was about ten minutes away. As the taxi drove through the busy streets they approached a well-designed building that was appealing in every way.

"I've booked us large rooms on the same floor," Wayne commented as the taxi slipped up to the entrance. "We'll be down the hall from each other so it will be easy to coordinate our activities."

"Great," said Olivia as they walked into the hotel, which was filled with people dressed for the evening, milling around. The place was spacious, well furnished, and had a lively atmosphere. It also looked expensive. Fortunately, Megan had suggested they stay there and put it on her tab.

"Nice place," Wayne commented as they entered. "We may even get time to jump into the pool for a quick swim."

Olivia smiled. It was nice having Wayne around to share the experience with, and of course to have his expertise as events unfolded.

"Why just the pool?" Olivia quipped. "Hopefully, we'll even get a chance to run to the beach and jump into the ocean."

"That would be amazing," Wayne agreed as they walked to the desk to register.

"We have a long day tomorrow," Olivia commented, thinking of the activities ahead of them.

"I think we should get up about eight or so," Wayne agreed. "We'll grab a quick breakfast downstairs in the hotel and then go over and talk to Bella. I'll make sure she knows we're coming."

This was certainly a change. Olivia was used to eating breakfast alone in her room, planning the day on her own. Things were going to be different now, she suddenly realized. She and Wayne were just starting out. They would have to find a routine and schedule that would suit both of them.

"Breakfast at eight sounds good," said Olivia.

"Want a quick nightcap now?" Wayne asked quickly, after their hotel registration was complete. "We can take some time at the bar to discuss our strategy."

Olivia smiled. That was as good an excuse as any, she thought, to take some extra time for a quick drink.

After they received the keys to their separate rooms, they left the lobby and slipped into a sleek bar a few steps away. It was surprisingly crowded, with soft lighting and slow jazz playing in the background.

"Good place to unwind," said Wayne as they took a couple of seats at a small cocktail table. "I like to unwind before I call it a night. Especially on a case like this. I don't have to tell you how intense the pressure can get."

"No, you don't," said Olivia. "I like it though." She realized things could become extremely heated, but it was better than a slow-paced life where she had plenty of time to think of all she'd been through. Working on cases, Olivia had no time to linger on memories of the past. Todd's horrible murder the night they got engaged, and the death of her first fiancé as well, receded into the background. She could throw herself completely into the problem at hand instead and make a real difference. It took the feeling of helplessness she had away. She was in charge now, no longer a victim. That felt not only good, but necessary.

The waiter came and Wayne ordered drinks and looked over at Olivia. "You don't seem at all tired," he mentioned, "even after all we've done today."

"I'm not," said Olivia. "In fact, I'm looking forward to the morning."

"To speaking to Bella?"

"Absolutely. There are huge gaps in this story that don't sit well with me."

"Like what?" Wayne was interested.

"Like why the cops are so focused on Megan, and Bella has completely slipped through the cracks. After all, Bella was the one there with Tyron. Megan wasn't."

"That's according to Megan," Wayne quickly replied. "Bella may have a completely different story."

The drinks came and Olivia took a long sip of hers. It was tangy and delicious. "What do you really have against Megan?" she couldn't help but ask Wayne.

For a second he looked put off. "I have nothing against her," Wayne finally said. "I just don't like young gals who marry old, rich fellas for their money. It doesn't sit well with me."

"You don't know for sure she married him just for his money," Olivia replied.

"Oh, come on. Why else?" said Wayne. "My sister was always money hungry too, and she's also married to a much older guy."

Olivia was surprised to hear that. "Really?"

"Yeah, they live way across the country, too," Wayne went on. "Pat used to be close to the family, but he grabbed her and took her to California. Now we barely hear from her anymore."

"That's not because he's older, though," Olivia commented.

"The entire situation is weird," said Wayne, "and I never could understand why she did it. I asked her a few times but she just clammed up."

"Maybe she loves him?" Olivia suggested.

Wayne made a strange face. "Sure, that's what she said, but that word love covers a host of emotions, doesn't it?"

"It can," Olivia agreed.

"It also covers a host of crimes," Wayne added.

"It's true," Olivia had to agree. She couldn't help thinking about what happened with her second fiancé, Todd. She thought of his profession of love for her when all along he was with someone else. That wasn't love, though, it was the profession of love. It was easy to get fooled, for sure.

Wayne finished the rest of his drink quickly, while Olivia just sipped hers. Wayne was more complicated than she'd realized. It was fascinating to learn new things about his life and how he'd responded to what had gone on.

"Now can I ask you the same question you asked me?" Wayne finally said. "How come you're on Megan's side? I know you and she are about the same age, but that can't be the reason."

"I'm not on anyone's side," Olivia responded.

"I actually find Megan to be cold to the core," Wayne added. "And hiring such an aggressive lawyer confirms what I think."

"I don't see it that way," said Olivia. "I think Megan's tough in her way, but what's wrong with that? And besides, her husband died suddenly. Cut her a break, for a little while anyway."

Wayne smiled. "I wish I could," he replied. "But that's not what we're here for. Whether or not she gets a break is not up to us."

CHAPTER FIVE

Olivia woke up early the next morning, showered, and dressed in a blue, summer-print silk dress. She then went down to the coffee shop of the hotel, where Wayne was already waiting for her.

When she walked in Wayne looked up and smiled, seemingly pleased to see her. "You're always on time, right to the minute," he said. "I love that about you."

"Thanks," said Olivia brightly, as Wayne got up and pulled out her chair.

"I was actually taking a bet with myself about whether or not you'd be here at eight sharp," Wayne continued.

"Did you win or lose?" laughed Olivia.

"Looks like I won," he said. It was good to be greeted so warmly and Olivia sat down feeling pleased. "I've ordered a pot of coffee for us for starters," he went on.

"I'll get some scrambled eggs and muffins," said Olivia, "and then we can be on our way."

"I'll have some too," Wayne agreed. As they waited for the waiter to come and take their orders, Wayne reached into his briefcase and pulled out some papers. "Here's some information I gathered about Bella last night after we went to our rooms," he said. "It's always good to be prepared before we actually go and meet someone in person."

"No question about that," said Olivia, interested. "What did you find out?"

"For starters, Bella is forty-five years old," Wayne began. "She's about fifteen years older than Megan, and she's been working for Tyron for almost ten years."

"Ten years?" Olivia was amazed. "That's a long time. Has he been sick for that long?"

"No," said Wayne. "It seems that Bella worked as a housekeeper before she became his personal aide."

"That's interesting," said Olivia. "Seems that Tyron knew her well and trusted her. When he got sick, it might have been natural that he wanted her to look after him."

"I would think that he would have needed a nurse," Wayne mused.

"Maybe he had a nurse in the beginning and this is just routine care," said Olivia.

"In any case, Bella knew Tyron before he married Megan," Wayne commented. "That's interesting and it's good to know."

"Yes, it is," Olivia agreed.

"Bella also had to know Tyron's first wife, Alice, and his daughters for quite a while too," Wayne added. "She must have been around during Tyron's divorce."

"Very possible," Olivia agreed. "This is important information for us. Bella can definitely give us a larger picture of what was going on in Tyron's life."

"If she's so inclined," Wayne reminded her. "If Bella wants us to know the whole truth."

The waiter came and they ordered breakfast as they finished their coffee.

"Did you find out what Bella's life is like outside of her job?" Olivia was curious and wanted to know more about her. "She's been working for Tyron since she was thirty-five. That's a long time. Does Bella have a life outside of work, of her own?"

"That's something we'll find out shortly," said Wayne. "It's a good question."

Breakfast came and as soon as it was over, Olivia and Wayne got up quickly to make their way over to Tyron's home. Right now both Bella and Megan were staying there. Olivia wondered if they were talking to each other at all.

*

Tyron's home was located at the end of a long road that led to a white, sandy beach. Located in the most exclusive part of Naples, the home sprawled grandly along the edge of the sand. The house had three floors, two outdoor patios, and a wooden walkway leading to the large, amber front door.

There was room to park down along the side of the walkway, and as their taxi pulled into it, Olivia felt a wave of anxiety. So much had taken place at this location and all the evidence had been collected by now. Olivia wondered how Megan and Bella were doing in there. Were they here alone? Had friends or family gathered around them?

After Olivia and Wayne got out of the taxi they walked up to the imposing doorway and rang the bell. To Olivia's surprise, almost as soon as the bell rang out, the front door flung open. A medium-height Latino woman with short hair, big shoulders, and peering eyes looked out at her. She was dressed simply in worn slacks and a loose-fitting shirt.

"Bella?" asked Olivia.

"Yes, of course. Who else?" the woman replied in a nervous tone. "Who else would be the one to open the door?"

"I'm sorry if we're too early," Wayne replied immediately.

"I'm used to it. I got up very early for Tyron every morning. How can I sleep anyway?" Bella hastily replied, opening the door further. "Come on in."

Olivia and Wayne slowly walked into the beautiful home. The main room was large and airy, furnished with a long, ivory sofa strewn with colorful throw cushions. The rugs on the floor looked handmade and plants and paintings perfectly complemented the décor.

"This is a beautiful home," Olivia mentioned as she looked around.

"Tyron only wanted everything beautiful around him," Bella replied. "If something was old, or used up, he'd say it was finished. I had to throw it out immediately."

Olivia cringed. Was that what happened with his first wife? Had she grown old, or used up, in his eyes? Had he begun to see Megan that way as well recently?

"Thank you for seeing us," Wayne said to her. "We need help from you."

"Everyone needs help from me." Bella put her hand up to her forehead. "Who do I go to for help myself?"

"We're here to help you as well," Olivia chimed in.

"No, you're not. I heard you're working for Megan," Bella replied.

"Megan hired us," Olivia went on. "But what we find out will help everybody, won't it?"

Bella smirked. "You never know, there's a lot to find out. Different people are going to have different things to say. The phone hasn't stopped ringing."

"Are reporters calling too?" asked Wayne.

"Everyone," Bella replied. "Megan won't pick up the phone right now. She's locked up there in her room speaking to no one except her lawyer and her best friend, Nellie."

"She's scared," Wayne breathed.

"That's putting it mildly." Bella looked at him quickly from under her heavy eyebrows.

"Are you sure of that?" asked Olivia.

"You can never be sure of anything with her," Bella snapped.

Olivia and Wayne looked at each other furtively.

"Come in, sit down, let's talk more." Bella suddenly let down her guard. Clearly, she'd decided she liked Olivia and Wayne. At least, she didn't distrust them.

Olivia and Wayne walked into the main room and sat on the couch, while Bella pulled up a chair beside them.

"Go ahead, ask me anything you want," Bella said then, a strange light in her eyes starting to shine.

"You told the police you were not with Tyron when he fell," Wayne started.

"I was in the kitchen peeling carrots, getting his dinner ready," Bella exclaimed. "I always prepared dinner for Tyron at exactly the same time. He always sat out there on the patio and waited."

"You've worked for him for a very long time," Olivia chimed in. She wanted to know more about Bella's life and her relationship to Tyron. "You two must have been close?"

Bella's lip curled at that word. "I don't know if I'd say we were close, but I definitely worked for him for a long time. Tyron gave me my first job when I came to this country. I'm a very hard worker and he liked that. He knew he could count on me, too. I was working for him when he got sick, so after his nurse left, I was the one he wanted to look after him."

"It wasn't too much for you?" asked Olivia.

"Of course not," said Bella. "If he needed a nurse, we called a nurse in. But by now he just needed someone to help him in and out of the wheelchair, dress him, get him his food. Nothing so difficult."

"It seems you're almost like a member of the family now," Wayne commented.

"What do you mean almost?" Bella turned gruff. "I took better care of him than all the others. I was the one he turned to, not them."

"Including his wife?" asked Olivia.

"Including everyone," Bella repeated. "It wasn't his wife's job to dress him and feed him. He didn't want that. Megan wasn't up to that either, and he knew it. Look, Tyron was a willful old guy. I'm not saying he was always easy to be with. He had his ways and wouldn't let them go."

"He drove people away from him?" Olivia asked.

"Sure he did. He could be hard to take." Bella stood up, agitated, and began pacing.

“He didn’t drive you away though.” Wayne stood up too and walked beside her. “Sounds like you were loyal to him, through and through.”

“He made it worth my while, if you know what I mean,” Bella quickly retorted. “I took good care of him and he returned the favor.”

“You mean he took good care of you financially?” Olivia got up and joined in.

Bella stopped pacing quickly. “Yes, he did,” she said. “Is that so bad? I sent most of the money home to the family and also used it to help my old aunt live.”

“No, it’s good that you helped out,” Olivia replied.

“I’m not saying every minute of my life here was wonderful.” Bella took a deep breath. “With Tyron, you had to pay back for everything he gave. There were no free lunches. He worked you hard.” Bella took a deep breath. “He always wanted a return on his money.”

“What do you think happened to him, Bella?” Olivia asked. “Was it some kind of a terrible accident? Could he have wheeled himself over to the edge of the steps and tried to get out?”

Bella guffawed. “Of course not, he couldn’t walk. He knew it. He wasn’t dumb.”

“What happened to him?” Wayne joined in then.

Bella shrugged painfully. “I don’t know,” she said in a suddenly ragged tone. “Talk to Megan and to his two daughters. They’re all spoiled silly. The daughters both hate Megan, too. Anything could have happened.”

“How does Megan feel about her stepdaughters?” Olivia asked.

To her surprise, Bella just laughed. “I wouldn’t call them her stepdaughters, no one does. We call them Tyron’s daughters. His ex-wife, Alice, is their mother. If Alice ever heard anyone calling her girls Megan’s stepdaughters, she’d have a fit. The girls are close to their mother, Alice. They can’t stand Megan, I told you.”

“What has all this got to do with their father’s death?” Olivia felt there could be a connection.

“I don’t know what anything has to do with anything.” Bella suddenly retreated like a turtle pulling back into its shell. “Talk to Megan and the girls. See what you think.”

“But you were the one who was here with Tyron!” Olivia intensified the pressure. “No one else was in the house but you and Megan. And she was upstairs.”

“So what?” Bella barked.

“It doesn’t look good for you,” Olivia added.

"This is a big house," Bella went on. "People come and go all the time and you never see or hear them. It's easy to get up on the deck in back. Anyone could have gotten up there and pushed him down the stairs!"

"Are you saying someone else got onto the deck with Tyron?" Wayne was all over it. "There's no physical evidence of that, no footprints or DNA."

"It's easy to wipe out evidence at the beach in the sand." Bella swiftly retreated again, her voice dimming. "I don't know who was or wasn't on the deck. I was in the kitchen, cutting carrots. When the police came they even found my carrot peels in the sink. When I went back out on the patio to tell Tyron dinner was ready, he was already face down on the sand. Face down! Someone pushed him! Why would it be me? There's no reason for it!"

At that Bella spun around, a look of fear and fury flashing over her tired face. Olivia wondered who Bella really was then. Did she have any other life of her own? Had Tyron completely consumed her? Could she have secretly wanted to break away?

"Where do you go on your day off, Bella?" Olivia asked.

"I stay with my aunt, not far from here," Bella glumly replied.

"Is there anyone else in your life at all?" Olivia continued.

"My job was my life," said Bella. "I was here six days a week, night and day. Tyron needed me, what could I do? "

"So, there's no one else in your life?" Wayne joined the line of questioning. "No special person of your own?"

Bella stamped her foot hard. "If I do or do not have somebody else in my life is no business of yours!" she suddenly barked, her face flushing. "And it has nothing to do with Tyron's death. If you want to know more about what happened to Tyron, talk to his two rotten daughters, Kayle and Lana. They're both going crazy now. They haven't stopped calling."

"We will," said Olivia.

"I'll go get their contact information right away," Bella added as she quickly stomped out of the room.

*

After Bella gave Olivia and Wayne the daughters' contact information, she made it clear the interview was over.

"I have things to do now," she said, motioning to the door.

"What kind of things?" Wayne was put off.

"I have to fix up the place, get some food ready, people will be coming soon."

“Who’s coming?” asked Olivia.

“People, all kinds of people,” Bella replied. “They want to come and pay their respects. Megan has friends and business associates and they’re coming to see her, too.”

Wayne nodded.

“Go talk to Tyron’s daughters,” Bella urged again.

“Are they coming soon, too?” asked Olivia.

“Might be,” Bella replied. “Call them and find out.”

CHAPTER SIX

Once outside the residence, Olivia and Wayne walked down toward the beach and stumbled upon a driftwood bench that had been placed unobtrusively under a tall, angular tree.

"Let's sit here for a few minutes," Olivia suggested. The sun was out in full force and the day was warm. But under the shade of the tree it was easy to feel the breezes rolling in from the ocean. They were refreshing.

"I think it would be best for you to call Kayle," Wayne said after they sat down. "It'll be less jarring for her to hear from a woman. See where she is and when we can get together. After that you can call her sister, Lana."

Olivia agreed. No time could be wasted and she immediately dialed the number Bella had given her. To her delight, Kayle picked up the moment the phone rang.

"What is it? What is it?" Kayle asked frantically before even knowing who was on the other end. "Did something else happen?"

"It's okay, nothing else happened. There's no emergency." Olivia tried to calm her. "This is Olivia Wells, the woman Megan hired to help sort things out for your family."

"The private investigator?" Kayle's voice rose a pitch.

"Yes," Olivia replied. "My partner and I are at your father's home now. We're gathering information."

"I'm on my way over there as we speak," Kayle answered quickly. "I couldn't go there before. Just couldn't. I've been up all night."

"I can understand that," Olivia said softly.

"Thank you," Kayle spoke a bit more softly.

"And how about your sister, Lana?" Olivia went on.

"What about Lana?" Kayle didn't like the question. "I know she's coming, but not sure exactly when. She spent last night with my mom in Fort Lauderdale. They were comforting each other."

"You weren't with them? Where did you spend the night?" asked Olivia quickly.

"I was with my fiancé, Drew," Kayle replied. "We live together about half an hour away from Naples. Drew's almost as shook up as I."

"Is Drew coming now too?" Olivia was interested.

"No, not now." Kayle began to sound breathless. "This first meeting at the house will be just for the family. We have a lot of things to talk over."

"Like what?" Olivia was interested. She hadn't known the family planned to meet at the house today.

"Like funeral and burial arrangements," Kayle said quickly. "Like the will, and our trusts."

It was amazing to Olivia that Tyron had barely died and they were already gathering to talk about practical matters.

"I hope I can speak to you when you arrive," Olivia continued.

"Of course you can," Kayle answered quickly. "Don't you think I want to help find my dad's killer?"

Olivia shivered. Kayle seemed so emphatic about his having been murdered. How could she be so sure? "His killer?" Olivia echoed.

"Well, my father didn't end up down on the sand on his own, did he?" Kayle shot back.

"It doesn't appear so," said Olivia.

"It sure doesn't. Just hold on a few more minutes," Kayle breathed. "Where are you, exactly? I'll be right there."

Olivia told Kayle where she and Wayne were sitting and hung up the phone. "Kayle's beside herself," Olivia said to Wayne. "She said she wants to help us find the killer. She's convinced her father was murdered."

"Good," Wayne replied. "If they didn't find any prints or DNA, whoever did this knew what they were doing. We're going to need all the help we can get."

*

In what seemed like a few minutes, a tall, slim, young woman with long blonde hair, a short skirt, and an open blouse came running down the pathway toward the driftwood bench.

"This has to be Kayle," Olivia murmured, standing up to greet her.

Kayle rushed right over to Olivia and grabbed her hands. "You're Olivia?" Kayle's eyes opened wide. "I thought you'd be much older. How long have you been a detective?"

"Long enough," Wayne answered, standing up and walking over to them.

"This is my partner, Wayne," Olivia introduced him.

Kayle's eyes quickly darted back and forth between them. "I read all about the two of you and your company when I found out that Megan hired you," she said. "I actually think it's fascinating."

"Would you like to sit down on the bench so we can talk?" asked Wayne.

"Why are we sitting on the bench?" Kayle looked nervous. "Why are we outside? Are we hiding from something or someone inside?"

"Who would we be hiding from?" asked Wayne.

Kayle smiled oddly. "Of course, you wouldn't be hiding from Megan because she hired you. But Bella might have kicked both of you out. She does that from time to time. Bella thinks she owns the place by now."

"Bella did suggest we leave for the moment," Olivia went on.

"I bet she gave you my number and my sister's too," Kayle commented.

"Yes, she did," said Olivia.

"It figures," said Kayle. "Neither Bella nor Megan can stand either of us. They'll do all they can to trip us up. At least they have that much in common."

"That's got to have been rough for you," Wayne commented.

Kayle took a moment to really look at him then. "Everything here has been rough for me for a very long time," she said. "How would you feel if your parent married someone the same age as you?"

"Not very good." Olivia empathized with her.

"It's creepy to the core," Kayle went on. "And Megan took every chance she could to rub it in. She'd show us the jewelry, clothes, and perfume my father bought her all the time. It hurt like hell to see it."

"Did he give you girls gifts as well?" asked Olivia.

"Rarely," said Kayle. "Once he married Megan, we were past tense. In his mind he associated us with our mother. Megan saw to that."

"I'm sorry about that," said Olivia.

"And you can imagine how he felt about my mom!" Kayle went on. "Once it was over it was over. He couldn't stand her anymore."

"Did you see your father often after the divorce?" asked Wayne.

"I did, my sister didn't," Kayle replied. "We never could see him alone either. Megan always had to be there, hovering around. She acted as if she were watching her precious treasure to make sure no one stole it away. She always had to keep a weird rift going between my dad and us."

"You must have been pretty angry with him," Olivia remarked.

"I was for a long time," Kayle agreed. "But once I met Drew I felt better about everything. Finally I had someone of my own. My father wasn't so important to me anymore. Finally, I could go to see him and not go home feeling torn up inside."

"Was your father happy about your engagement, at least?" Olivia continued. "Was he going to make you a beautiful wedding?"

"Sure, he said he'd make a wedding," Kayle replied glumly. "And then, as soon as he said it, he started making lists of all the people he was going to invite. The wedding was for him, not for me. He wanted to look good in front of the world. That really upset Drew, too. He kept saying we should run away and elope. We should have a tiny wedding without my father at it."

"Drew hated your father?" Wayne jumped in.

"No, he didn't hate him," said Kayle. "Hate is much too strong a word for it. Drew's an independent guy who doesn't need fanfare. And he doesn't like to be told what to do."

"You and Drew are happy together?" Olivia wanted to hear about it one more time.

"Sure we're happy." Kayle's face grew red as she spoke. "Drew's a good guy even though he's not ambitious. He's nothing like my dad. That can be grating at times, too. We could definitely use some more money right now."

Olivia looked at Wayne, who was listening closely to every word.

"Well, you must have quite an inheritance coming now," Wayne murmured.

Kayle stopped talking then and stared at Wayne openly. "You better believe it!" she insisted. "And I can use every penny I can get."

Wayne shuddered. Kayle had no idea she had just handed them a clear-cut motive for the murder, Olivia thought.

"How about your sister, Lana? Does she need money badly now, as well?" asked Olivia.

Kayle backed up and looked away. "Lana always needs something badly," she said. "But she's not planning an engagement right now, if that's what you're asking. In fact, she just broke up with her boyfriend of two years about a month ago."

"Sorry about that," said Olivia.

"No, it's good that she's finally out of the lousy relationship. Charles was a rotten guy, through and through. He was only with her to get what he could. He was nasty to my sister, too. When my father finally didn't cough up what Charles expected, he backed out. His relationship with my sister wasn't going to give him the easy ride he'd hoped for."

"Sounds like Charles did your sister a big favor to get the hell away," Wayne commented.

"Yeah, he did, but she still can't see it for herself," Kayle said. "Lana feels like both he and my father betrayed her. She feels my father is the reason Charles left."

"When will Lana be here?" asked Olivia.

"She's on the way," said Kayle. "She left Ft. Lauderdale this morning. My mother's planning on coming up soon, too."

"A regular family reunion," Wayne murmured, as a car drew up to the front house and parked.

In a few minutes a lovely young woman with flaming red hair got out of the car. She was dressed in a navy denim dress with a large, glittery bag slung over her shoulder.

"That's Lana?" asked Olivia.

"That's her," said Kayle. "It's strange to see her. We actually haven't seen each other for about two months." Kayle began waving at Lana then. "We're here, Lana. Down under the tree."

Lana threw a long glance toward them and headed down the path. "What are you doing here?" she sputtered as she arrived close up at the bench. "Why aren't you inside with Megan and Bella?"

"Why should I be?" Kayle shrugged.

"Well, I'd imagine Megan would be devastated and need some company," Lana breathed.

Kayle looked startled. "Why would you think that? When has Megan wanted us around before?"

Lana paused and looked at her sister. Lana's eyes were blurry and red. It looked as if she'd been crying.

"This isn't before," Lana answered slowly. "Dad is gone now. Everything's different."

"Megan isn't different, though," Kayle quipped.

"Had do you know that?" asked Lana.

"I don't for sure, but don't expect anything like that." Kayle seemed irritated by her sister. "Don't expect us all to become one happy, cozy family now."

Lana breathed out feverishly and sat down on the bench. "Who said we were going to become a happy, cozy family?" she echoed. "Even now you have a way of making everything worse."

Kayle bristled. "I'm just trying to keep things real," she said. "This isn't time for hopeless fantasies."

"Are you suggesting I live with hopeless fantasies?" Lana jumped up, offended.

"Sometimes," Kayle breathed softly.

"You're referring to my relationship with Charles?" Lana confronted her sister. "Well, he's gone now and I hope you're glad about that. Charles is gone and you are engaged!"

Kayle's face reddened. "Are you accusing me of something? Is it my fault that you stayed with Charles for so long? Is there something wrong with my getting engaged?"

The tension between the sisters was quickly growing and Olivia felt she had to intervene.

"Right after the loss of a loved one, it's easy for everything to get out of perspective," Olivia said. "But this is the time you need each other."

Lana turned on Olivia full force. "Don't tell us who we do or do not need," she fumed. "That's not what you're here for. You're here to find our father's killer. And to find him fast."

Olivia was startled by the intense bitterness in Lana's tone.

"You're right," Olivia answered quickly. "I was just trying to tone things down."

"That's not your job," Lana repeated as Wayne took a few steps toward both of them.

"We'd like to talk to you alone, Lana," he said calmly. "That would be helpful. Is it possible?"

"Sure, it's possible." Lana turned her back to Olivia and faced Wayne. "You want to talk to me alone yourself?"

"With my partner, Olivia," Wayne responded.

"If we have to include her, we do," Lana shot back. "But I'd rather talk to you alone."

Wayne threw Olivia an inquiring glance over Lana's shoulder, but Olivia shook her head no. She not only needed to be present for the interview with Lana, but thought it would be a good thing that Lana felt shook up by her. The more shook up she was, the more she'd spill.

"Let's all go back into the house," Olivia suggested lightly, "and we'll continue our discussions in there."

CHAPTER SEVEN

It was cooler inside, shaded and breezy with large overhead fans turned on. The moment they entered the house Kayle immediately headed to another wing.

"Where are you going?" Olivia asked, uneasy.

"I'm going to find either Megan or Bella," she said. "I'll leave you two alone with Lana. I'm sure Lana prefers it that way."

"I do," replied Lana cryptically. "For starters, anyway."

"Fine," said Kayle. "We can talk more later on when you're ready."

Kayle left and Lana breathed a sigh of relief. "Kayle's always been a handful. I just can't deal with her right now."

Olivia was surprised. She'd found Kayle to be straightforward and interesting.

"How is Kayle a handful?" Olivia asked.

Lana turned away and looked at Wayne as she replied. "Kayle always has a derogatory comment about everyone she meets. I've never heard her say she's grateful for anything. And Kayle hung onto my father like glue after the divorce, even though he treated my mother like poison. My mother never got over that."

"How did your father treat your mother like poison?" Olivia chimed in, even though Lana refused to meet her glance.

"My father dumped my mother for a woman half her age. Megan was the same age as her daughters and he shamed my mother in front of everybody," Lana spit out. "She had no idea it was coming either. When my father told her she fell apart, stayed curled up in bed for months crying. I remember those days as if they were yesterday."

"That's rough," Wayne agreed.

"All my father said to her then was 'Get over it, sweetheart. Straighten up! I'm not coming back!'"

"Did your mother think your father would come back one day?" asked Olivia.

"Of course she did," said Lana. "My mother thought he was going through a crazy fling and it would definitely end. It never did though. Not ever."

"There had to be trouble in their relationship before that happened?" Olivia inquired.

Lana spun back around and stared at Olivia. "Yeah, big trouble. My mother got older, that was about it. My dad always liked to have something new and shiny. He wanted the latest version of every toy."

"Did your father take good care of your mother financially when they divorced at least?" Wayne asked softly.

"Sure, he gave her money," said Lana. "He had to, of course. But my mother was still in love with him. And she was the mother of his daughters. She'd been at his side at all his huge events and parties. Her life had been everything she'd always dreamed of. People looked up to her then. After the marriage ended, people backed away. She barely got a call from anybody. My father took her entire life away."

"It all ended just like that," Olivia echoed.

"Just like that!" said Lana. "There was no warning at all! One day my mother woke up and my father told her to pack up."

"There had to be a warning sign," Wayne spoke emphatically. "Something had to have happened."

"That's right, something happened." Lana faced Wayne again. "One night, out of the blue, at a party he hosted, Megan appeared. Without a second's hesitation, she walked right up to him, put her hands on his shoulders, and said, 'You're mine.' It happened in a flash. My mother told me the story many times. And a friend of my mother's was there when it happened. She saw it all in front of her eyes."

There was something missing in the story, Olivia felt. It didn't make sense.

"My mother's friend said Megan was young, sexy, beautiful, and my dad was transfixed. He couldn't take his eyes off her and she wouldn't take her hands off him. He was spellbound."

"Then what happened?" Olivia wanted more.

"In a short time my parents' marriage was over. Very soon after that he married Megan. Not only that, she insisted they have a big, flashy wedding. It was the talk of the town. Every time there was an article about it, or someone mentioned it, my mother crumbled again."

"That had to be very hard on you, too," Olivia commented.

"Hard is putting it mildly," said Lana. "And it was much harder on me than on Kayle, who took it for what it was worth. She just shrugged and said, these things happen. In lots of ways Kayle is like my dad. But her attitude hurt my mom a lot. And, to top it off, she kept going to visit my dad and Megan regularly."

"Was he good to Kayle when she went to visit?" Wayne was fascinated.

"Not really," Lana replied. "My dad and Megan put up with her for a little while, then they told her they were busy. It didn't matter, Kayle kept coming back to see them time after time. It was almost out of spite, if you asked me."

"She wanted something from him," said Olivia.

"Kayle told me she refused to lose her father," Lana answered. "She said she wouldn't let Megan push her out."

"What's your mother's life like now?" Wayne changed the topic.

Lana suddenly perked up, "Well, believe it or not, my mother's finally remarried! It actually happened about six months ago. No one could believe it either. A couple of years ago she suddenly had enough. She started working out and dating. My mom's a really pretty woman and lots of guys were interested. Finally, she met Clay. They've been married now for about six months."

"That's recent," Wayne noted.

"It's not only recent, it's odd too," Lana continued. "Clay's also much younger than my mom! I think she did it to get back at my father if you really want to know. Clay's young, good-looking, a hot commodity. He teaches scuba diving, is a sculptor, and never made much money. And my mother's loaded. So, figure it out."

Olivia shivered. Lana's comment didn't make her feel good about this new marriage.

"Your mom will be even more loaded now that your father has died, won't she?" Olivia asked.

Lana made a sour face. "My father doesn't owe my mother anything financially now. What he does with the rest of his money is totally up to him. Of course everyone expects that Megan will get the lion's share of the estate. But you never know, my father can be funny. He likes to play games. How do we know he wasn't also getting tired of Megan and decided to leave his money to someone else?"

"Like who?" asked Wayne abruptly.

"Like us, his daughters," Lana quipped. "That's what I'm hoping, anyway. I'm hoping he came to his senses and decided to do right by his family after all these years."

"Why would he do that now?" Wayne was curious.

"You never know," said Lana. "My father was really disturbed when he found out that my mother was marrying such a younger man. He made all kinds of comments about it and even asked her not to. He said it made her look foolish. Naturally, my mom just laughed in his face."

"Could your father have had buyer's remorse?" Wayne questioned. "Did he want his original family back?"

"Doubtful," Lana answered. "Having her original family back was my mother's dream though, for a long time. And she tried to make it happen over and over. She'd dress up and go speak to my dad, try to make him come to his senses. But there was no hope. Megan had him firmly in her grip."

"Your mother must have felt very rejected," Olivia replied.

"Of course! She was, and she never got used to it," Lana exploded. "We were all very happy when she found Clay."

"Your father became less important to her then?" asked Wayne.

"Maybe?" said Lana. "I'm not positive. And I'm also not positive what my dad's life with Megan has really been like recently. Bella's told me a bunch of stories."

"Tell us," Wayne said, eagerly.

"No, they're just stories," Lana insisted. "I'm not getting pulled in. Go to Bella and get her to tell you herself."

"All right," Wayne agreed. "Olivia and I will go right now."

Olivia thought it was a good suggestion and was about to get up to go speak to Bella again when the front door suddenly burst open. An attractive, middle-aged blonde woman, dressed in a crimson summer dress, burst in. She had a small suitcase with her and seemed to be on the edge of tears.

"Mom!" Lana burst out.

"I got here quicker than I thought," the woman exclaimed, rushing over to Lana.

"So glad you did," replied Lana before turning to Olivia and Wayne. "This is my mother, Alice," she said.

Alice pivoted toward Olivia and Wayne. "Who are you?" she spoke feverishly.

"They're the private investigators that Megan hired," Lana quickly filled in.

Alice ran her hands through her thick, wavy hair. "Tyron hasn't even been gone for two days and the place is already crawling with cops looking to dig up the dirt on him. Well, get ready, there's plenty of dirt!"

"Megan hired them instantly," Lana went on, "and she also hired Cameron Fern."

"I heard about Cameron," Alice replied, "but not the detectives. The detectives make sense, but not a barracuda lawyer like her. What's the point?"

"Sounds like Megan expects trouble." Wayne entered the conversation.

Alice smiled at him. "Megan lives off trouble," she whispered. "She can't get enough of it. I have no idea what else she has up her sleeve. No one does. She's full of tricks. Be careful."

"Sounds like you hate her," Olivia suddenly joined in.

Alice trembled for a moment. "Do I hate her?" She echoed the word. "I did for a long time, of course. I don't hate her as much these days. She's been with my husband a long time, though, and I'm sure by now she's gotten plenty of his flack. Tyron's very rich and he uses his money to manipulate everybody. I'm sure he did it with Megan, too. It couldn't have been all wine and roses for her, living with my husband all those years."

"Tyron has been Megan's husband for quite a while," Olivia reminded Alice.

"In a manner of speaking," Alice scoffed. "But I'd definitely say the first wife is the real wife! After all, I'm the one who had his children! I'm the one who raised them, not her. I didn't come on board later for the good times to play!"

"It's Tyron you hate then?" Wayne took up the questioning.

"Hate's not the right word," Alice objected. "Tyron's the one I felt worried about. He's been trapped in Megan's clutches for too long. I knew it would end badly one day. It had to."

"End like this? Through his death?" asked Wayne.

"Why not?" Alice swirled toward him. She was exceptionally attractive and fiery for a woman her age, thought Olivia. "If you're asking if I thought Tyron's life would end with him being murdered, I would say no," Alice went on. "I thought his disease would eventually get him. He got sick a few years into his marriage. I always wondered about that, too."

"You thought Megan had something to do with it?" Olivia confronted Alice directly.

"Anything's possible, isn't it?" asked Alice. "I even mentioned it to Tyron, but he scoffed at the idea. Then I realized it was divine justice and that he got exactly what he deserved." Alice paused. "There's always divine justice. Do you believe it?" She addressed the question to Olivia.

"I do," Olivia replied, wanting to go back to the main point of the conversation. "You thought Megan wanted him dead and was killing Tyron slowly?"

Alice looked at Olivia with fire in her eyes. "Why not? She would stand to receive plenty of money when he died, wouldn't she?"

"Are you suggesting Megan was killing Tyron slowly?" Olivia wanted to be sure of what she was hearing.

"You have no proof of anything like that though, do you?" Wayne added.

"No, not proof," Alice spoke harshly. "But over the past years when I went to visit Tyron I noticed him becoming more and more dizzy. Was Megan was poisoning him, I wondered, or was a tumor growing inside his brain?"

Olivia looked at Wayne. "The medical examiner's report will answer all those questions," Olivia responded professionally.

"If Tyron was growing more and more dizzy then it's even possible he just fell out of his wheelchair down the steps and onto the sand. Isn't it?" Wayne suggested.

Alice shook her head back and forth violently. "No, impossible," she insisted. "There's no question but that someone pushed him down the stairs onto the sand. It was something I was afraid of for years." She went over then and sat down on a small settee and put her head in her hands. "Oh my God, he's gone, he's gone," she began moaning. "I'm never going to see him again."

Lana rushed over to her mother. "It's all right, Mom, it will all work out."

"But he's gone," Alice continued, "and that horrible monster Megan is now going to get every penny he's worth."

"We're not sure of that yet," Lana breathed forcefully. "Nothing's certain."

Olivia also wanted to comfort Alice, but wasn't sure how to. "You're remarried now, though, aren't you?" she finally asked, stepping closer.

Alice stopped moaning abruptly and looked up at her. "Yes, I am, so what?"

"I mean it's not as if you're all alone now," Olivia replied.

"Of course I'm alone." Alice looked forlorn. "I've been alone since the day Tyron threw me away, discarded me! Wiped me out! You never get over something like that. And how dare you bring in my marriage at a time like this? I had a right to get remarried."

"Of course you did." Olivia didn't want any misunderstandings. "But now you're not alone."

"There are different levels of being alone," Alice answered heatedly. "Of course, Clay keeps me company, why shouldn't he? But he doesn't replace Tyron. And it doesn't mean Tyron and I aren't still connected. After all, I'm the mother of Tyron's children. Clay is recent, and he's younger than me. There are things we share and lots we don't. It's completely different."

"No one is suggesting you don't have a history with Tyron," Olivia replied. "No one is suggesting there isn't a reason to grieve for him."

Alice was suddenly filled with fury. "There's a divine justice in this universe," she repeated.

"Of course there is," Olivia agreed. "But what does that have to do with you and Tyron?"

Just as Alice was about to reply, Wayne's cell phone rang loudly, interrupting them.

Wayne immediately picked up. "Yes, yes, I see," Wayne answered quickly. "Well, that's good news. I'm glad you called. Olivia and I will come to the station immediately."

"What's up?" Alice, unsettled, walked over to him.

"The police have the surveillance video now and have gone over it. They want us to come right over and take a look," Wayne replied.

"It sounds important," Alice exclaimed, nervously. "It sounds as if they found something." Alice's words tumbled over one another. "Did they see someone else in the house at the time?"

"That's the question, isn't it?" Olivia chimed in. "And very soon we'll have the answer."

CHAPTER EIGHT

Olivia was relieved to be out of the house and on the way to the police station with Wayne. The day had grown warmer and her head was spinning after talking to Alice and her daughters.

"Quite a family!" Olivia commented as their taxi drove to their destination.

"Quicksilver, all of them," Wayne replied, "including Megan and Bella. You see one thing one minute, something else the next."

"We definitely need more time with both Megan and Bella," Olivia noted. "I'm actually surprised that Megan wasn't downstairs, milling around, waiting to talk to us."

"We'll get all the time we need," Wayne replied. "This family meeting that's about to take place is going to be jarring. They'll probably all be at each other's throats. Megan must be preparing for it."

"I can see why she hired such a tough lawyer," Olivia commented. "Without doubt Tyron's estate will be contested."

"It's pretty ugly to think a person's life comes down to this," said Wayne.

The thought of it saddened Olivia, as well.

"But it's one thing if Tyron died of natural causes," Wayne continued, "and something else entirely if he was murdered." The taxi stopped in front of the police station and Wayne leaned over to pay the fare.

"Especially if someone in the family killed him," Olivia couldn't help but add.

"If Tyron was killed by someone he left money to, then his inheritance would definitely be up for grabs," Wayne quickly filled in. "But very often the dead person has the last laugh. When the will is read you find that they haven't left their money to anyone in the family at all. It's their last revenge. Their money goes to someone entirely unexpected. Sometimes it's a secret relationship no one knew about."

"Then all breaks loose, I'm sure," Olivia murmured.

"It definitely can," Wayne agreed.

Olivia and Wayne got out of the taxi, walked into the police station and then down the long hall to the main office. They knocked on the door briskly.

"Come in," James Gallant called out. "Door's open."

Wayne opened the door and they entered. Two other officers were there as well, sitting around a long table with Chief of Police James Gallant. Olivia recognized Marcus from the first time they arrived, but didn't recall seeing the other one.

The other officer stood up and smiled at them. "Ed Mahoney," he introduced himself.

"Ed specializes in working with surveillance video reconstruction," Marcus offered.

"Wonderful," said Olivia. Ed was young and slender with sharp, blue eyes. She liked him immediately.

"I hope you found something in the video that will turn things around," Wayne remarked.

Ed smiled at Wayne and shook his head slowly. "I wish I had too, but it's complicated," he replied.

"We'll play the video for both of you," Gallant offered. "You see for yourself what you think. Then we can go over our conclusions."

Ed walked over to a screen opposite the table while Olivia and Wayne took their seats. After he pulled the shades down and the room grew dark, he switched on the video quickly. There was a long humming sound as the picture slowly came up on the screen. At first there was nothing but a blur, then a few wavy figures appeared.

"What's that?" asked Olivia.

"Not really sure," Ed responded. "It could be anything. We can't even be exactly sure what time or day this was taken."

"It looks as though there are a few people in the background, doesn't it?" Olivia leaned closer to the screen.

Wayne immediately stood up. "Not at all! It doesn't look like anything! This video's clearly been tampered with."

"Exactly," Ed agreed. "The humming noise and the wavy lines give it away completely. The evidence has been tampered with!"

"Oh my," breathed Olivia. "Were there other cameras at the front or back of the house?"

"One other at the front of the house," Marcus joined in. "This particular video was kept on the back patio to monitor Tyron. Seems he sat out there alone a lot. If Bella or Megan were somewhere else in the house, they would then be able to see him.

And if he needed them, he rang a bell he had close by, so he could reach them."

"Perfectly orchestrated," Gallant murmured. "And not only that, upon closer examination of the premises we discovered that Megan could have easily seen what was happening to Tyron all the time. The window in her upstairs office looked right down onto the back deck. It's actually quite likely that she was an eyewitness to his death."

"Wow," breathed Olivia. "And what about Bella?"

"She claims she was in the kitchen the whole time," Gallant replied.

"Tyron must have rung the bell for her when there was trouble out there," Olivia jumped in.

"If he had time to, he might have," Marcus jumped in. "If he wasn't taken unaware."

"What about the surveillance video in the front of the house? Any help?" Wayne joined in.

"That one's blurry too, but easier to make out. They're working with it right now at headquarters. As soon as it's ready they'll let us take a look."

"The basic point is that with what we have here, there's no way to know exactly what happened to him," Gallant exclaimed. "There's no hard evidence yet."

Ed wasn't comfortable with that conclusion. "We do know that this back surveillance video was definitely tampered with though," he declared. "That itself is evidence of foul play."

The room grew quiet for a moment.

"There were no fingerprints on the video?" Olivia asked quietly.

"I only wish there were." Ed smiled at Olivia. "But whoever did this planned each step carefully. It wasn't an amateur, that's for sure."

Ed shut off the video and went back to the windows to pull the blinds open. A harsh sunlight filled the room.

"If you asked me"—Gallant took over the discussion then—"I would say that the tampering with the video points to Megan, more than anyone else. She was a resident of the home and would have been most likely to know how it worked. "

"Why not Bella?" Olivia interrupted. "She was the one caring for Tyron."

Everyone turned to Olivia, surprised. It seemed as if Megan was the suspect the group favored at the moment.

"We're not ruling Bella out," Gallant countered quickly. "But what possible motive could she have? She worked for Tyron for years and needed the salary. And, from what I hear from those checking the front surveillance video, they think they can see Bella in the kitchen cooking when Tyron was killed."

"Isn't it possible there are other videos somewhere that have been taken down or hidden?" Wayne broke in then.

"We're searching for them, of course," Marcus responded. "Oftentimes they turn up, but as of now they haven't."

"Megan's the one with motive." Gallant picked up where he left off, addressing his words to Olivia. "You've heard of black widows, haven't you?"

Olivia nodded. This was the second time that idea had been mentioned.

"We get a lot of them down these ways," Gallant went on. "Young girls hungry for older guys' money. They're determined to get it too, any way they can."

"Thieves," Olivia mouthed.

"And sometimes violent killers," Gallant continued. "That scenario makes sense to me in this case."

"No. It's way too early to say that." Wayne raised his hand as if to hold back the accusations.

"I know Megan's the one who hired you," Gallant continued. "But you've got to stay open about this. You two could be the perfect cover-up for her."

Wayne wasn't averse to the suggestion. "The idea's crossed my mind," he mentioned. "Don't worry though, I've been in the business for too long to let something like that happen."

Gallant seemed relieved. "Good," he said. "Because as of now, it's not looking good for your client."

"We plan to explore this further," Olivia chimed in as Gallant smiled at her.

"Great," Gallant emphasized. "It's a pleasure to have two honest, open-minded detectives to work with, no matter how it turns out."

*

When Olivia and Wayne left the station it was too hot to walk outdoors in the streets.

"Let's get out of here and go somewhere shady with breezes," Olivia said spontaneously.

"How about the Botanical Gardens?" Wayne perked up. "There's plenty of shade there and it's a gorgeous nature preserve."

"Wonderful." Olivia felt relieved by the idea of it. She needed time in a new environment. It would help to go over what they had so far, and decide where they were headed.

Rather than take a taxi, Olivia and Wayne jumped on the air-conditioned trolley that drove through the city on its way to the Gardens.

It was fun gazing out the windows at the flashy town. They passed along streets filled with expensive shops, beautiful cafes, and charming restaurants. At the end of the line the trolley turned straight into the renowned Botanical Gardens.

*

The Botanical Gardens was a welcome shelter from the heat, filled with trails, tropical gardens, and beautiful trees.

After they entered and walked along a bit, Olivia and Wayne seated themselves under an old tree with large, waving branches. Fortunately, a breeze had blown up and as they enjoyed its coolness, they were surrounded by an incredible array of flowers in every hue. It was uplifting to be seated in the midst of nature with its unspoiled beauty.

"This was a great idea," Wayne said as they settled in. "Nothing like some downtime to recoup and decide our best next steps."

"I agree," said Olivia, pleased to have Wayne there to go over everything with. It was a totally different experience working with a partner rather than taking on a case alone. Olivia loved it. She felt supported, challenged, and able to harness resources she might not have had access to before. Olivia learned a lot from Wayne and respected the way he interacted with others.

"It seems like they've all decided that Megan's the culprit," Olivia commented.

"It's not unusual to latch onto an initial person of interest," Wayne replied. "That's a common way to launch an investigation. Besides, what else do they have right now? Nothing, really."

"It's not good to be skewed so early on, though," Olivia replied. "Once you focus entirely on one person other clues are easily bypassed. Aren't they?"

"True," said Wayne, smiling. "How'd you get so good at this?"

Olivia smiled along with him. "I guess it's always been natural, in my bones."

"That's for sure," Wayne agreed. "But I'm also sensing that you really don't think Megan did it. Do you?"

"Somehow I don't," Olivia replied. "I'm keeping my options open, though."

"You have to," Wayne implored. "And that's what I like so much about you. You want what's right. You keep your mind open. That's exactly what got me into this work as well. Fairness and justice. Even when I was a little kid I couldn't stand to see the wrong person accused of doing something he didn't."

"Who did you see accused when you were little?" Olivia loved it when Wayne told her more about his life.

"Nothing terrible," Wayne continued. "I saw kids accused in school, fights on the playground. My mother always jumped to accuse my little brother Tim when he and I got into a fight. Even when I told her I was the one to blame, she kept accusing him. It bothered me."

"Of course it would," said Olivia. "And what did Tim do then?"

"He would just cry." Wayne looked upset at the thought of it. "Tim could never defend himself very well, and my mother knew it."

The story touched and troubled Olivia. She hadn't realized the full extent of how kind Wayne was.

"That's awful for your brother," she continued. "Did he outgrow it? Did he grow stronger?"

"Not really," Wayne replied. "Tim's okay now, but he still can't stand up for himself."

"So you're doing it for him now, and for the whole world," Olivia exclaimed.

Wayne looked startled by her comment. "I never thought of it that way," he said quietly.

"That's beautiful, Wayne," Olivia continued. "We all have incredible reasons for doing what we do. Most of us have no idea about what most of our reasons are either."

"That's for sure," Wayne couldn't help agreeing.

Wayne stood up then and took a few steps away. Olivia wondered if her comment may have been shocking for him. Or perhaps the conversation was too close for comfort. She stood up then as well.

"It would be good to get moving," said Wayne then, running his hands over his face. "How about taking a walk on the hiking trails?"

"Sure," said Olivia, "let's go."

They started walking away from the bench down to a beautiful trail. Surrounded by trees and large bushes, the trail was home to many little birds which flew happily overhead. It was cool and refreshing here too, good to be walking.

They walked along in silence for a while. “What’s next in the investigation?” Olivia asked, wanting to get back on focus and have a plan in place by the time the trail ended.

“I was just thinking about that.” Wayne picked it right up. “Obviously we have to look more deeply into Megan’s background and also Tyron’s finances. I’ll dig into the finances and you see what you can find out about Megan’s life.”

“Good plan,” Olivia agreed as they suddenly arrived at the end of the trail.

“I just want you to know how much I appreciate working with you,” Wayne said suddenly as they approached the front gate. “I learn something new every day.”

Olivia felt grateful. “Me, too,” she replied. “We’re a good team, Wayne.”

“You can say that again,” he replied. “Definitely.”

CHAPTER NINE

After leaving the Botanical Gardens, Olivia and Wayne drove by Tyron's home. The place was bustling, with many members of his family and close friends gathering. Olivia knew they were there to prepare for the funeral, memorial, and burial. The outside of the home was surrounded by reporters, looking for a slice of the story that had taken South Florida by surprise. Every news station was carrying recent developments. Along with the reporters, sightseers stood snapping photos for mementos.

"Should we stop and go in?" Wayne asked as they drove by.

"Not right now," said Olivia. At the moment Olivia felt her picture of Megan was skewed by others, and informed by rumors. She decided that before she met with Megan again in person, Olivia wanted to gather more background information about her. It would be best to work from the quiet of her hotel room, she thought.

"I'd rather go back to the hotel and do some research first," Olivia continued. "It's quiet there, I'll be able to think."

"Good idea," Wayne agreed. "I'll start researching Tyron's business dealings in my room as well."

When they arrived at the hotel Olivia went into her room, while Wayne walked down the hallway into his. She felt both relieved to be alone for a while and also glad that he was close by. Olivia imagined that Wayne felt the same way as well. They seemed to be on the same page about most things.

Olivia took her computer out onto the patio of her room. Thankfully, it was cooler by now, as the light of the day had faded. Still, there was enough light to see clearly and Olivia scrolled from one site to another, pulling up articles about Megan and her background and her wonderful, unexpected marriage to Tyron Barr.

As Olivia scrolled through the information, she suddenly stopped cold at the sight of a broken link to an article about Megan. What was this piece about? Why was it taken down? On a whim Olivia quickly put a call in to the publication to find out more.

After being connected to one person after another at the publication, Olivia finally hit gold.

"Can you find the article that the broken link leads to?" Olivia pleaded. "This is a police investigation."

"I'll look," the woman responded nervously.

Olivia waited for a few moments until the woman spoke again. "Yes, I see the article you're talking about," she finally replied. "It's about Megan Barr. It seems her husband, Tyron, paid to have the piece taken down."

Olivia shivered. This was more important than she'd realized. "Thank you so much," she breathed. "Please tell me what the piece is about."

"Well, I'm not sure I can," the woman faltered.

"This is important," Olivia interrupted. "I'm investigating a possible homicide and your cooperation is essential."

The woman's voice lowered. "I see," she replied.

"The case is all over the news, I'm sure you've heard about it," Olivia pressed her.

"Yes, I have," the woman acquiesced. "It seems it's a long article about Megan Barr that was written about her at the time of her marriage to Tyron and printed in the society columns."

"Read it to me," Olivia demanded.

Without hesitation, the woman continued. "The headline says, 'Beautiful Rag-Tag Model and Escort Nabs Older Rich Tycoon.'"

"Rag-tag model and escort?" Olivia was stunned. "Are they referring to Megan Barr?"

"Yes, they are," answered the woman. "It says that originally, Megan came from a poor home on the other side of the tracks. As she grew older and more beautiful, she worked both as a model and an escort."

An escort? Olivia wondered. Was that a nice word for a high-class call girl?

"Megan met Tyron through her work," the woman continued somberly. "A few girls from her agency had been invited to spice up a party he was throwing. The girls were there for his clients, of course. However, the night Megan attended something entirely different happened. Tyron himself became the object of her attentions. The two of them were instantly inseparable. The rest was history!"

History, indeed, thought Olivia. "Thank you so much," she said to the woman. "You've helped a great deal."

"It's my pleasure," said the woman. "Should I send the article to you?"

"Yes, you must," Olivia replied before she hung up.

It took a while for Olivia to absorb all she'd just heard. Alice had told Olivia that Megan and Tyron met at one of his parties. She neglected to mention, however, that Megan was a paid escort.

Perhaps Alice felt that would have made her look even worse. Olivia thought about the networking parties that Megan now ran. Who was she introducing to whom? Was this a continuation of the work she used to be in? None of this looked good for her in any way. Nothing did. But why would Megan continue to run these parties? She certainly didn't need the money. Olivia realized she'd have to talk not only to Megan, but to the people she interacted with. Hopefully, they might see her and her past from a different point of view.

As Olivia sat there musing, there was a light knock on her door. She got up, went in, and opened up.

Wayne stood there, smiling . "Time for dinner?" he asked as he strolled inside.

Olivia hadn't realized how much time had passed already. "Sure, why not?" she said.

"We can order up into the room," Wayne continued, "and talk about what we found."

Wayne called down for dinner quickly and then joined Olivia on the patio. A few stars were beginning to shine in the sky as the darkness descended.

"From what I can see," Wayne started, "Tyron had a complicated life. All kinds of money and business involvements."

"Aren't the police looking into that?" Olivia asked. "I'd think his business involvements would be the first thing they'd dig into."

"Sure, they're looking," Wayne agreed, "except they can only spend so much time and money on it. A labyrinth like the one Tyron was involved in requires a full-time person to decipher."

Olivia was fascinated. "What kind of labyrinth? Shady investments?"

"That's putting it mildly," said Wayne. "He seems to have had hidden investments in all kinds of firms. The more you look the harder they are to decipher. My guess is that he had a large group of people indebted to him."

"You're saying that something went sour with one of his investments?" Olivia asked. "Was there someone who couldn't pay him back? Did they take him out because of it?"

"That's always a possibility, of course," said Wayne. "Tyron could have been putting pressure on somebody. Right now that's just speculation, of course. It's worth looking into though. I'm doing it."

"Good," said Olivia. "From what I found, Tyron looked after his clients beautifully. He ran all kinds of parties to keep them happy. Even hired models and escorts to spice up the night!"

Wayne grinned. "That's a common practice down here," he said. "The girls are perks for the clients."

Olivia got up and walked to the edge of the patio. Wayne took the escorts lightly and that bothered her. She turned and looked at him directly.

"Did you know that Megan was one of the perks, as well?" Olivia added.

That grabbed Wayne. "Really?"

"Yes, Megan worked for the escort agency Tyron hired for the party the night they met."

Wayne kept grinning. "Now that's something to discover!"

"Not only was Megan a model and escort," Olivia went on, "as soon as she got to the party, she promptly seduced Tyron. The article said that the rest was history."

Wayne laughed. Olivia wasn't sure why he was laughing. "Tyron was married to Alice when he met Megan," she went on, irritated. Olivia was hoping to see some outrage in Wayne, but there was none.

"Yeah, I'm sure he was," Wayne remarked flippantly. "Things like that happen all the time."

"You're not bothered by it?" Olivia felt out of sorts. Why wasn't Wayne registering disturbance about something like that?

"No, not especially," Wayne answered. "I've seen it too often, it's par for the course."

"It's not par for my course," Olivia shot back, wondering if maybe that was why Wayne was still single. "It's not good to take things like this casually," she went on. "It could affect your own life and relationships."

Wayne bristled. "What are you getting at?"

The doorbell rang then. "Probably the waiter bringing dinner," Olivia commented.

Wayne got up and walked into the room, opened the door, and pulled in the dinner tray. It bothered Olivia that Wayne took Tyron's infidelity so lightly. What did that tell her about Wayne, his values, and how he felt about relationships?

"Should I bring the food out there?" Wayne called.

"Whatever you like," said Olivia.

Wayne slowly wheeled the tray out onto the patio and took out their dinner plates. After their dinner was set up on the small table, he returned to the question he'd asked a few moments ago.

"What do you mean that my attitude towards Tyron could be affecting my relationships?" Wayne asked.

Olivia was surprised that he brought it up again. Obviously, her comment had bothered him.

"I was surprised by your reaction to Tyron's infidelity, as if it didn't matter much," she said.

"Everything matters in its own way," Wayne responded. "I just don't get bent out of shape by things I see every day. But what did you mean that my attitude could be affecting my relationships now? Are you wondering if that's why I'm single?"

Olivia felt put on the spot. "Maybe," she said quietly. "Maybe your attitude has hurt your trust in relationships."

Wayne grew silent a moment. "I haven't always been single," he went on. "Actually, I was in a long, very good relationship. We meant a lot to each other."

"I'm sorry," Olivia said suddenly.

"Carey was killed suddenly in a car accident," Wayne continued. "A car blew a stop sign and smashed right into her. Everyone said she never knew what happened."

Olivia's stomach clenched. "That's awful," she gasped. "I had no idea."

"But I wasn't so sure whether or not she knew what was happening or not. I was a few feet away and saw it all happen." Wayne spoke woodenly, now. "It wasn't all as simple as it seemed. From where I stood I thought she could have seen the car coming. She stayed at the stop sign for too long. Did she stay there too long on purpose? Did she do this to herself?"

Olivia felt alarmed. "Had Carey been depressed?"

"I didn't think so," Wayne continued, "but she was definitely quieter than usual the past few weeks before. I didn't say anything to her about it either."

"You think she took her own life?" Olivia felt awful for him.

"I'm not sure," Wayne replied. "It's not so simple to say."

"It never is," said Olivia.

"But it still hurts like hell," Wayne added.

"Of course it does," Olivia echoed. "And it makes it worse to blame yourself."

"Hard not to in these kinds of circumstances," said Wayne.

Olivia felt a chill rise through her. She had no idea Wayne had been through something like this. "I'm truly, truly sorry to hear this," she offered.

Wayne took a few steps closer to her then. "I know you are," he said. "I know you only want the best for me."

"Of course," Olivia concurred. She looked at their dinner getting cold and was about to say something when the phone rang. Fortunately it broke the tension of the moment.

"I'll get it," Wayne said abruptly.

He picked up, said hello, and listened to the speaker on the other end for a few minutes.

"Fine," said Wayne, suddenly. "Yes, of course, we'll check into it further."

"Who was that?" asked Olivia when he hung up.

"The medical examiner's report is in," Wayne announced.

"So fast?" Olivia was jarred.

"Tyron died as a result of a blood clot that burst on the brain," Wayne continued. "They've concluded that the event was most likely due to his fall. For the moment that puts the cause of his death in the realm of accident. There's no hard evidence yet of anything else."

"No evidence of his being pushed? No fingerprints on him?" Olivia checked.

"No, nothing like that," Wayne replied, "and no substances in his body. The killer certainly knew how to cover their tracks."

"Could it have been an accident?" Olivia wondered. "Could someone near him have accidentally pushed him?"

"Doesn't make sense," said Wayne.

"No, of course not," agreed Olivia. "No sign of any other drugs in his body?"

"No, nothing at all," Wayne added. "The police, however, are asking us to investigate his medical condition further. Why don't you go talk to Tyron's doctor and find out if it was possible for him to stand from his wheelchair or attempt to. But before you go to the doctor, go talk to Megan. We need to stay in closer touch with her."

Olivia agreed. "I was actually planning to talk to her first thing in the morning," she said. "I'll do that and then go see Tyron's doctor."

"Good," Wayne rallied. "And now it looks like our dinner might be growing cold." He threw a light glance at the food laid out on the table beside them. "Are you still up for eating?"

"Of course," said Olivia. "Why wouldn't I be? Cold or not, let's enjoy."

*

After dinner Wayne left and Olivia went back out onto the patio. She stood there alone for a long while, looking out at the dark sky. Wayne had been open and honest about himself with her and she appreciated that. There was never any way of knowing what a person had been through. It was shocking for her to hear about his girlfriend and all the pain he'd undergone.

Olivia couldn't help think about her own life as well now, about how sideswiped she'd been by Todd. Olivia thought of the time she'd found out that Todd had been seeing another woman just as they were getting engaged. His declarations of love had meant nothing. He'd convinced Olivia utterly, though; she'd thought every word he'd said was true. Now Olivia had difficulty trusting her own judgment with men. How could she have been so blinded? Olivia wondered, as she stood here alone.

Olivia thought of her relationship with Wayne now. She and Wayne had both retreated into their work, for different reasons, but in the same way. Being a detective was incredibly demanding and forced you not to dwell on the past. When you were part of an investigation you entered someone else's life and had to be incredibly alert to what was going on. There was no time or space left for anything else. Was there a way to build a life of your own as a detective? Olivia wondered. Many did, but Olivia had no idea how.

CHAPTER TEN

To Olivia's surprise Megan was not willing to talk to her first thing in the morning. "Come later in the afternoon," Megan said, in a hushed tone. "There are too many people here now, too much I'm dealing with. I need quiet in the mornings, anyway. I can't talk the minute I get up."

"Okay," Olivia agreed, deciding to first go see Tyron's doctor and find out more about his physical condition and any other information the doctor might have.

Olivia called and to her delight, Dr. Anguil made time for her immediately. His nurse mentioned that they realized this was urgent and would move their schedule around.

"Come right over," said the nurse. "We'll be waiting."

Olivia left right away and quickly arrived at Dr. Anguil's well-furnished office, set in a home off the main road under a trellis of large flowers. As soon as she knocked, his nurse opened the door.

"Olivia Wells?" the nurse asked immediately. "Please come in."

The nurse ushered Olivia into a large, airy waiting room that felt more like a porch. A few magazines were scattered on the long coffee table, but other than that the room was empty.

"Dr. Anguil will be with you in a few moments. He's delighted you decided to come and speak with him," the nurse commented as Olivia looked around. "And he's always on time. Just finishing up with the patient before you."

"I'm grateful that he's taking time to speak with me," Olivia replied.

"Of course, we're all extremely shaken by the sudden loss of Tyron." The nurse suddenly looked down at the floor.

Olivia detected something strange in her tone. "I can only imagine," she replied.

The nurse started to leave but Olivia stopped her. "Tyron's death was completely unexpected, of course?" Olivia continued.

The nurse looked up swiftly and gave Olivia a knowing glance. "For most people it was," she barely replied.

"And for you?" Olivia was glued to the woman.

The nurse met Olivia's glance. "I never felt Tyron was entirely safe," she answered in a low, hoarse tone.

"Why not?" Olivia took a step closer to her.

"I'm not sure, I don't know. Perhaps it was because he couldn't get out of that wheelchair."

"But he had someone caring for him all the time, didn't he?" Olivia remarked.

"Yes, that's true, but it's a vulnerable position nevertheless." The nurse's voice grew louder.

"Is that the only reason he wasn't safe?" Olivia couldn't let it go at that.

"I don't know, I'm not sure," the nurse repeated. "But if you want the absolute, complete truth, I wasn't as surprised as everyone else by the news!"

That was important and Olivia needed to know more about it. "You expected Tyron to come to harm?"

"I wouldn't say I expected it," the nurse corrected her. "But it didn't surprise me either."

"Do you know more about Tyron's life?" Olivia took another step closer.

At that the nurse backed away. "No, I don't, not really. Only what I read in the papers like everyone else. I never spoke to him personally, he barely noticed me at all."

At that moment the door to Dr. Anguil's office opened and a woman in a linen suit hurriedly left. After that Dr. Anguil, a tall, heavyset man with salt and pepper hair stepped out of his office.

"Thank you for coming to see me." He extended a large, warm hand to Olivia.

Olivia took his hand and shook it. "I'm grateful for your time and cooperation as well," she replied.

Dr. Anguil then turned around and motioned to Olivia to follow him. They walked a few steps along a hallway to his large, immaculate office and went in. Once inside he took a seat behind his big, square desk.

"We were delighted to hear that private investigators were on the case," he started. "The police have only so much time and resources. And this case is complicated."

Olivia was pleased to hear that, taking his comments as an invitation to jump into the heart of the matter.

"As Tyron's physician," she started, "I assume you had no reason to believe he was close to death?"

"Absolutely not," Dr. Anguil said firmly. "In fact, just the opposite was true. I thought Tyron was doing quite well recently, given the restrictions he was living with."

"What was wrong with him, exactly?" asked Olivia bluntly.

"He had a neurological disorder that intensified," Dr. Anguil replied. "As is common knowledge, he could no longer walk or get out of his wheelchair alone."

"He was suffering from a progressive illness?" Olivia asked.

"Yes, but I had kept him stable for a long while." Dr. Anguil spoke vehemently now. "There was no indication that things had advanced at all." Dr. Anguil's tone displayed the deep upset he was dealing with.

Olivia wondered if she should ask about Dr. Anguil's personal relationship to Tyron, but decided to keep it entirely professional. "I'm interested in the onset of Tyron's illness," Olivia said then. "What were the causes?"

Dr. Anguil gave Olivia a long glance. "The actual cause of his neurological disorder is unknown, of course. Some would say it was genetic, others attribute it to the aging process. Many are afflicted with it. In some it goes slowly, in others advances fast. Some remain mobile with it, others not. Fortunately, in Tyron's case we were able to manage the course of his illness. Although he was no longer ambulatory, he was not in significant pain. The quality of his life was quite good, too, I would say."

"Especially married to such a young, beautiful wife." Olivia smiled, wanting to know more about the relationship.

Dr. Anguil did not smile in return.

Olivia returned to the previous point. "Is there any chance his illness was brought on by someone, or by something given to him?" she asked.

"There is no evidence of that at all," Dr. Anguil replied. "I also heard that there was nothing in the medical examiner's report to suggest foreign substances or drugs in his body."

"No, there wasn't," Olivia agreed.

"Naturally, one cannot help but wonder about things like that," Dr. Anguil finally said slowly, offering Olivia quiet encouragement.

Olivia was grateful for his comment. "Yes, it was important to rule that out," she agreed. "If Tyron was doing well recently, there was obviously no indication that he had a blood clot in his brain, was there?" She needed to explore every possibility.

"There was no indication of that at all!" Dr. Anguil stood up swiftly. "In fact, Tyron had a recent MRI of the brain. No blood clot at all."

"So the bleed in his brain that killed him had to be a direct result of the fall?" Olivia confirmed.

"It definitely looks that way." Dr. Anguil's face tightened. "Tyron's head hit the rock he landed on fiercely. As he fell down a flight of rather high steps the blow was intense."

"There was no way he could have gotten out of his wheelchair himself and tried to get downstairs?" Olivia checked once again.

"No, of course not, that's preposterous," Dr. Anguil assured her. "Tyron was completely clear-minded. He knew what he was doing every second of the day. He also knew what he needed and wanted. When he came here to see me, he always let me know everything that was happening in his life."

"What was happening?" asked Olivia, fascinated.

Dr. Anguil walked back and sat down at his desk. "I mean everything that was happening medically, that is."

"He was well cared for at all times, I assume." Olivia continued probing. Dr. Anguil wouldn't step over the medical boundary. He didn't dare go near anything personal in Tyron's life.

"Yes, of course, he was beautifully cared for." Dr. Anguil became somewhat restless now. "He came here for medical checkups regularly and had an aide with him continually. His every need was met."

"He was fortunate in that respect," Olivia commented.

"In that respect, yes, I agree," said Dr. Anguil.

Olivia and the doctor looked at each other a long time then. Olivia realized that Dr. Anguil had to respect the privacy laws. He was limited in what he could and would tell her. She'd try one more time to get more information from him.

"Did Megan ever come with him for a visit?" Olivia asked then.

"Not that I recall," he replied.

Olivia grew quieter. There was no need to go round and round. She could finish this interview promptly.

"Dr. Anguil, in your professional opinion would you say that Tyron was definitely pushed down the stairs?" Olivia asked.

"There's no question at all in my mind," he gruffly replied.

"And, just for the record, do you have any idea at all about who could have done something like this?"

"That question is beyond my scope," he said. "I can speculate like everyone else, of course. But it would be pure speculation. What I can say without any question, though, is that from a medical point of view Tyron was definitely pushed."

After thanking Dr. Anguil again, Olivia left the office and walked slowly back out onto the street under his front trellis. She felt spurred on by their meeting. Even though the information he could give her was limited, Dr. Anguil was plain, direct, and honest. It was absolutely clear now to Olivia that Tyron had definitely been pushed. It would now be up to her and Wayne to find out why and by whom.

Once out on the street, Olivia looked at her watch. It was already late morning. Megan would have had plenty of time to get up and be ready to talk. Olivia put in a quick call to her and to Olivia's relief, Megan was not only ready to see Olivia, but seemed glad of the opportunity.

"Meet me at Wilmer's coffee shop, down near the pier," Megan answered quickly.

Olivia was surprised they weren't meeting at her home.

"I can't stand it here in the house, I have to get out," Megan continued. "There's a regular dragnet that's forming here. It's suffocating me."

"I'll be at Wilmer's in about twenty minutes," said Olivia.

"Fine," said Megan, "I'll see you there."

*

Wilmer's coffee place was one of many charming restaurants and cafes lining the pier. It was close to the ocean and Olivia felt good being down there, out of the main rush of town. It was quieter and the light breeze from the ocean was deeply refreshing.

The moment she walked into Wilmer's, to Olivia's surprise Megan was standing at the door, dressed in a light golden summer dress, her long, beautiful hair tied back off her shoulders. Her eyes looked blurry and tired, though. Once again Olivia was startled to see how young Megan was; they could have been friends in school.

"Thanks for coming down here," Megan said immediately, grabbing Olivia's hands.

"No problem, I like it here," Olivia replied quickly.

"I still can't get over how young you are," Megan answered, looking Olivia over.

"Don't worry, I can do this job," Olivia replied.

Megan stared at her then. "I sure hope you can because they're all closing in on me now."

"Let's sit down and talk," said Olivia, leading Megan to a quiet, roomy booth in the back.

Once they sat down, Megan quickly pulled her hair loose and let it fall over her shoulders and face. For a second she looked wildly distraught.

"Who's closing in on you, Megan?" Olivia started.

"The usual suspects." Megan looked up at the ceiling. "Tyron's hideous family who hate my guts. They've always hated my guts, and naturally it's worse now."

"You mean Tyron's ex-wife and daughters?" asked Olivia.

"That's right," Megan snapped. "They've camped out at the house now, without even asking me if that would be okay! They're acting as if the place and everything in it belongs to them now!"

"It doesn't," said Olivia. "Can you ask them to go?"

"No, I can't," Megan shot back. "That would only make me look worse in their eyes. Then I turn back into the evil stepmother. They're all walking around downstairs, talking about Tyron constantly. I've heard they're even going to invite their friends over soon."

Olivia was startled to see how helpless Megan really felt.

"I did tell them that I don't want them to invite all their friends over," Megan said. "They say they're doing it to plan for the funeral and memorial. Alice, his ex-wife, seems to think she's still married to him! She always did."

"She's remarried though, hasn't she?" said Olivia.

"How do you know that already?" Megan's head shot up.

"I talked to Alice and Kayle and Lana," Olivia replied.

Megan froze up. "You don't miss a beat, do you?" she asked.

"I can't, time is short," said Olivia. "If we want to find out what really happened, we have to move fast."

"Why?" Megan looked alarmed.

"Evidence has a way of disappearing or being hidden quickly," said Olivia.

"Who would be hiding it?" Megan gasped. She seemed completely distraught and Olivia could understand now why she'd hired a tough lawyer.

"Is your lawyer around? Is she helping you out?" Olivia continued.

"We're in touch every day," said Megan. "She'll be around more when the will gets contested. She's not a criminal lawyer, but she advised me to lay low."

"What does that mean, exactly?"

"It means to realize anyone could have done it, and to keep my mouth shut. It means they're all going to try to bait me and make it look like it's me. I can't respond to any of that. My lawyer said it's all a trap."

Olivia listened carefully. "That's good advice," she replied. "What do you think happened to Tyron, Megan?"

"I already gave you some possibilities the first time we met," said Megan. "Check Bella, the ex-wife, and his horrible daughters."

"Wayne and I have," Olivia replied.

"Check them more," Megan insisted. "We're all having a meeting to plan for funeral arrangements at the house this afternoon. Come over and join in. You'll see another side of them all. You'll hear things you never could have imagined. Something new could be revealed."

The waiter came to take an order, but neither of them could eat. Olivia just ordered some coffee for herself and Megan.

"You guys have no real evidence yet of anything, though, do you?" Megan suddenly asked.

"If you mean hard evidence, forensic evidence, no, not yet," said Olivia.

To Olivia's surprise, Megan smiled, relieved.

"Don't you want us to find real, hard evidence?" Olivia asked, suddenly wondering if Megan was covering something up.

"I don't know what I want anymore," Megan answered. "Right now I just want this to be over. Then I want to sell the damn house and get away from this life I've been living. I want to get as far out of town as I can."

Olivia shivered. "You run networking parties here, don't you?" Olivia needed more information.

"Yes, of course I do, why?" said Megan.

"Who are you introducing to whom exactly?" Olivia asked pointedly.

"What do you mean by that question?" Megan took exception.

"Who are your clientele? It's important," Olivia continued.

Megan stood up swiftly. "Are you accusing me too, now? Are you suggesting I'm into something rotten? Did you find out about my lousy past? Are you holding it against me?"

"No, I just need to know." Olivia stood up as well.

"Go to hell." Megan looked as if she were going to slap Olivia.

"I'm here for you, Megan," Olivia insisted. "I just need to know the whole story."

"No, you're not here for me, you're not," Megan cried out. "But for your lousy information, I run networking parties for entrepreneurs, business people starting up small businesses, who need the support of each other. They need contacts and feel alone. I actually love what I do."

"Okay," said Olivia, surprised. "That's good, it's great, I needed to know that."

"No, you didn't!" Megan flared up again. "You wanted to know if I was still an escort, didn't you? You thought I could be pimping for the girls. Confess! That's what you were thinking, wasn't it?"

Olivia decided to be straightforward. This wasn't a time to play games. "That thought did pass my mind," she responded. "If that's what you were doing, I needed to know."

Megan immediately fell silent. "Well, thank you at least for being honest with me," she replied. "I appreciate honesty, I need it."

"So do I," said Olivia.

"Well, for your information, yes, I'm still in touch with some escorts. Why shouldn't I be? They were my good friends. I've known them for a long time. Is there something wrong with that?"

"I didn't say there was," Olivia murmured.

"And just because we're friends," Megan continued, "that doesn't make me one of them!"

"No, it doesn't," Olivia agreed.

"They're good girls, too. I like them," Megan continued petulantly. "They're definitely much better than Kayle and Lana, any day."

Olivia grew silent. "I'd love to meet some of these friends, if I could," she replied.

"When the time is right," said Megan. "For now, just come to the house this afternoon for the family meeting. And bring your sidekick with you." Megan suddenly smiled.

"My sidekick? You mean Wayne?" asked Olivia.

"Yeah, who else?" Megan laughed. "I liked him when I met him. He's cute."

Olivia was startled that Megan noticed another man's attractiveness so soon after her husband had died. What did that say about her marriage to Tyron? It might well have been over a long time ago. For all Olivia even knew Megan could be really happy that he was finally gone. What if all this time Olivia had been getting behind a woman who was guilty?

"Of course my partner will come with me," Olivia remarked offhandedly.

"Good." Megan liked that. "And I'll bring my sidekick, too, my lawyer, Cameron."

CHAPTER ELEVEN

The family meeting at Tyron's home was shaping up to be a bombshell, thought Olivia. She told Wayne he absolutely had to attend with her. Everybody was going to be there.

"I wouldn't miss it," Wayne quickly agreed. He'd been busy digging into all kinds of records of Tyron's assorted business dealings, looking for that one contact who might have been holding a vendetta against him.

"Great," Olivia replied. She was particularly glad Wayne would be coming along. Her meeting with Megan had been unsettling. Olivia had felt somewhat frightened in the beginning, but as she spent more time with her, Olivia felt sad for Megan as well.

"How did your meeting with Megan go?" Wayne now asked over the phone.

"It was complicated," Olivia replied. "I'll tell you when we see each other in person. I'd love your take on Megan after this afternoon's meeting, too."

"Fine," agreed Wayne. "I'll meet you at Tyron's home a few minutes before the meeting begins."

Olivia hung up feeling relieved and supported. As the days went on it became clearer to her how much this work was really a group effort. All hands had to be on deck. All eyes had to look at circumstances from their own point of view. Then each one had something unique to contribute to the puzzle they were trying to put together.

*

As always, when Olivia arrived at Tyron's home, Wayne was outside waiting, exactly on time. Standing under a nearby tree, wearing a light blue summer jacket and a checked shirt, he looked especially handsome. Olivia had also dressed for the occasion, wearing a beige summer suit and a lovely print blouse.

"Wow, don't you look snazzy," Wayne said as Olivia approached.

"I was thinking exactly the same thing about you." Olivia smiled.

Pleased, Wayne pointed to the house. "Should we make our grand entrance?"

To her surprise, Olivia felt apprehensive. "Let's go," she said.

When they got to the front door, it was open and they just walked in. The moment Olivia entered the large entrance foyer, her apprehension intensified. The tension in the air was palpable and the sound of people talking and stirring in the next room had an abrasive feel to it.

"We're walking into trouble," she whispered to Wayne as they turned toward the large side room where the meeting was obviously taking place.

"Why else would we be here if there wasn't trouble?" he whispered back.

Olivia and Wayne entered the room, which was filled with people. Many were walking around, talking to each other and holding cups of coffee. Megan was standing in the far corner, talking heatedly with a tall, stunning woman who was dressed to the gills. Along with her flashy, expensive jewelry, the woman's hair was perfectly coiffed. She certainly seemed formidable.

"Whew, that's some woman Megan's talking to," Wayne remarked, noticing her immediately.

"It must be her lawyer, Cameron Fern," Olivia replied.

"I'd sure like to know what they're talking about so heatedly," said Wayne.

"Let's go find out." Olivia was right on it. She suddenly remembered how Megan had asked her to bring Wayne along, saying how much she liked him. Olivia decided not to tell Wayne about it at the moment. It was better for him to stay neutral, not caught in the web of the feelings flying all around.

Olivia and Wayne waded through the crowded room toward Megan. From the corner of her eye Olivia saw Kayle in another corner, a handsome guy standing beside her. That had to be her fiancé, Drew. Kayle's sister, Lana, was in another corner, talking to an older man. Olivia wondered where Alice was. She scanned the room briefly, but she wasn't there.

When Olivia and Wayne got closer, Megan turned on her heel, saw them, and immediately stopped talking to the woman.

"You're here, finally!" Megan said, swiftly.

"This is the time the meeting was called for, wasn't it?" Wayne responded.

Megan smiled. "Yes, it is. I wasn't suggesting that you were late. I was just looking forward to introducing you to my lawyer, Cameron Fern."

Cameron took a step toward them and extended her beautifully manicured hand. "So pleased to meet both of you," she said. "Megan obviously needs all the support she can get."

"The three of you are my team today," Megan interjected. "I know you won't let them mow me down."

"No one is mowing you down, Megan," Olivia responded. It was important to hold onto reality, not get swept away by fears.

Cameron spun toward Olivia angrily. "You have no way of knowing whether or not someone here wants to mow Megan down, do you?" she remarked. "From where I'm standing Megan is entirely in her rights to make that request and express those feelings."

"I never suggested that Megan wasn't within her rights." Olivia stood up for herself in a flash. "I'm trying to say that there's no evidence of anyone being out to get her yet."

"The very worst possible thing you can do is blame the victim." Cameron cut into Olivia's comments. "Blaming the victim is actually a way of disempowering them and shutting them up."

Wayne stepped in strongly then. "Olivia isn't blaming anyone," he said, trying to set Cameron straight. "Olivia's just trying to defuse the situation. When things calm down, we can all see clearly what's really happening."

Cameron took well to Wayne's comment and smiled at him unexpectedly.

"Okay, you win," she said more softly. "But in case you don't realize it, you actually sound like Olivia's guardian angel, protecting her from me."

Olivia bristled and was about to reply when Wayne continued. "Olivia can handle whatever she needs to on her own."

"Really?" Cameron flushed a bit and stepped closer to him. "Please don't take my comments the wrong way. It's delightful to see a man who is a rescuer. You don't see it much anymore these days. I only meant to say I was impressed with you." Cameron ran her hand through her hair lightly.

Olivia flushed, watching Cameron openly flirt with Wayne. Thankfully, Wayne didn't take the bait. He had no part of it. Olivia felt enormously relieved.

"This isn't about me," Wayne responded to Cameron. "It's about Megan. We're all here for her."

"Well put," Olivia chimed in, trying to put Cameron in her place.

"Okay, okay." Megan waved her hands. "The meeting is starting in about three minutes. Let's go over to the couches and sit down. Kayle is running the meeting and she has an agenda set up for us all to go through."

"Why is Kayle in charge?" asked Olivia.

"Because she's the favored daughter!" Cameron quipped. "Kayle's claiming she's the one in the family who was closest to her father! They're all obviously trying to shove Megan out the door."

"Let them try all they want." Megan gritted her teeth now. "It's all going to backfire on them all, believe me. I've been up against tigers before."

Olivia, Wayne, Megan, and Cameron then walked to the center of the crowded room and sat together on one of the long leather couches. Cameron managed to sit close up, next to Wayne, and Megan took the spot beside Olivia. All of them sitting there together felt like a lineup to Olivia.

"Okay, okay." Kayle rang a little hand bell. She was standing in front of the room, dressed in a long, black cotton dress and simple sandals. Actually, Kayle looked more like the grieving widow than Megan, thought Olivia.

"We have a lot to go over before the funeral," Kayle spoke in a loud voice. "I really thank everyone for coming. Please take your seats."

"Why didn't you insist on running the meeting?" Olivia whispered to Megan, who trembled slightly beside her.

"I wasn't up for it," Megan whispered back. "I didn't want to stand there and be a public target of their hatred and insinuations. Would you?"

"Now that the autopsy has been done and the medical examiner's report is in, we must decide on disposal of the body," Kayle started.

Olivia was horrified to hear her put it so clinically.

"Megan has stated that she wants my dad to be cremated immediately," Kayle announced to all. "And I definitively oppose the idea."

A strange silence fell over the room.

"I personally want to wait until there's further investigation of the crime," Kayle continued.

"The autopsy is complete." Cameron stood up then and joined the discussion. "The body has no relevance now in the investigation."

Kayle flushed and stepped forward. "It has relevance for me! It's my father!" she declared as Lana ran up to the front of the room to stand beside her.

"It's my father as well," Lana joined in. "And I totally agree with Kayle."

Kayle looked relieved and pleased by the unexpected support. "Who knows what we'll find if the body is investigated further?" Lana added.

At that Wayne stood up as well. "The autopsy has been done by a top medical examiner," he said. "There is nothing else to find."

"You don't know that! Something else could be hidden," Kayle insisted in a shrill tone. "Why is Megan in such a hurry to reduce my father to ashes?"

Megan put her head in her hands as Cameron then spoke up again.

"You are publicly making negative assumptions and implications about my client!" she announced. "Cremation is a normal procedure after the autopsy has been completed."

Despite the tension between them, Olivia couldn't help but be impressed with Cameron. She was a staunch advocate for Megan, refused to allow her to be maligned.

"Where is Mom? Where is she?" Kayle turned to Lana then. "Let's hear what she has to say about the burial."

"Mom's been rummaging through papers upstairs," Lana replied. "She'll be here any minute. She told me she's already found something and is looking for more."

Olivia wondered what Alice had found and how it would impact the discussion.

"We are asking everyone in the room to support us in our decision," Kayle spoke to the crowd that had gathered. Olivia wondered then who all these people were. Were they family, friends, Tyron's business acquaintances? Had Kayle purposely gathered them together as a wall of resistance against Megan's wishes?

Megan stood up suddenly as if a strong wind had hit her. "This is all ridiculous," she shouted. "I am the wife here and what happens to my husband's body is up to me! And me only!"

"Not when there's a criminal investigation going on," Lana shot back quickly.

"There's not a criminal investigation going on." Megan's voice got louder. "The results of the autopsy said Tyron's death was an accident!"

The room fell totally silent once again. Olivia realized, of course, that medically there was no evidence of Tyron's being pushed, so they had to call his death an accident. But given the fact Tyron could not move on his own, the presumption that he'd been pushed was clear to all concerned. The case had to continue being investigated so they could determine who did it.

Megan walked up front to Kayle and Lana.

"There's no way my father's death could have been an accident and you know it!" Lana hissed at her.

"This is not a criminal investigation!" Megan repeated in a harsher tone. "And if it ever became one, there would be plenty of suspects around!"

Kayle took Megan's comment badly. "Oh really? Just what are you implying?"

"I'm not implying, I'm saying that I am the wife here and the decision about cremation is up to me!"

"Why are you in such a hurry to destroy my father?" Lana chimed in then. "Tell us why."

"The funeral is tomorrow!" Megan began yelling. "Decisions about burial have to be made now."

At that Alice suddenly burst into the room and frantically ran up to her daughters and Megan.

"Where were you, Mom?" Lana grabbed her mother's shoulders. "We've started already."

"I'm sorry I'm late," Alice breathed, "I didn't realize the meeting had started already."

"Megan's insisting that Dad be cremated," Kayle spoke in a shrill tone. "We're refusing her request."

"Not only are you simply refusing." Alice grabbed a paper out of her bag. "I have a statement right here that Dad wrote a long time ago. It clearly states that he did not want to be cremated, ever!"

A palpable gasp was heard in the room then.

"I always remembered hearing Tyron say that to me," Alice continued. "As soon as I heard that Megan wanted him cremated, I started frantically searching for proof. I found it! Here it is!" Alice waved the piece of paper in her hand. "I was looking for more statements like this. But at least I have this one."

Cameron rushed up to the front of the room then and grabbed the paper out of Alice's hand.

"This statement has to be fully corroborated and substantiated, of course," Cameron declared. "We have to be sure you didn't just forge it."

"How dare you accuse me of forgery?" Alice's face grew red.

"Not accusing, just suggesting it's a possibility, isn't it?" Cameron was on a roll. "But at the very least, you've succeeded in delaying the cremation now!"

The room fell silent once again.

"I've succeeded in assisting the investigation!" Alice spit back. Then she spun toward Megan. "Tyron didn't fall on his own and we all know it! Someone had to have pushed him. Someone who was there, in the house! It wasn't Bella either, why would it be? She took care of him for years!"

Megan grew pale and taut. "Who are you? My judge and jury?" she flung back.

"I'm Tyron's first wife! I'm his real wife," Alice shouted as the room began murmuring. A few were standing up from their chairs, when suddenly a strong, handsome young man burst into the room.

"Cut it out! Stop this!" he called.

"Who's that?" Olivia asked Wayne.

"I refuse to let this go on," the young man continued, rushing up to the front. "Stop it, Alice. This is not right."

"Back off, Clay," Alice demanded.

"That's her new husband," Wayne murmured, stunned.

Clay jumped between Megan and Alice. "This is enough," he repeated. "Things have gotten out of control."

To Olivia's amazement, Megan dropped her head and began sobbing.

"What are you doing defending a killer?" Alice stared at him. "Why are you taking her side against me?"

"Nobody knows what happened yet!" Clay insisted. "You can't accuse Megan. She's suffering too."

"Megan's a killer!" Alice hissed at him.

But Clay would have none of it. "You're all in shock. No one has the right to say that anyone is a killer now."

"This is one good man," Wayne murmured.

"How dare you defend Megan?" Alice turned to him heatedly. "You're my husband! Mine!"

"I'm defending fairness and truth," Clay continued.

"Oh really?" Alice sneered. "So who else could have pushed Tyron, then? You tell me!"

"That's for the police to find out, and the detectives." Clay tried to calm Alice down. Olivia was stunned that Clay was Alice's new husband. He was so young and vital and they seemed so ill suited in every way.

"This is Alice's husband?" Olivia said to Wayne.

Clay turned to everyone. "Okay, let's all pause a moment."

"For now it seems we'll hold off on arrangements for the burial," Alice cut him off. "We can go on tomorrow with the funeral until a final decision has been made." Alice seemed victorious as Megan turned away, flushed.

Megan ran over to Olivia then and pulled her aside. "See, I told you, it's a dragnet forming," she whispered.

"Clay's not a part of it though," Olivia couldn't help but comment.

"No, he's not. He's a decent guy," Megan quickly agreed. "He's the only one here who cares about the truth. In fact, he helped me find a video no one has seen yet. It was on a video surveillance camera, taken a few weeks ago. Bella's on it, screaming at Tyron. I told you, she secretly hated his guts."

Olivia was shocked. "Why didn't you tell me before?"

"I was waiting for us to be alone," said Megan. "I didn't want to tell you in front of Cameron. I have to be careful what I tell her and when. Cameron has a short trigger. I didn't want the information becoming public too soon."

"That's wise," Olivia agreed.

"Can you and Wayne come and look at the video after the meeting?" Megan asked desperately. "It could be the piece of evidence that turns everything around."

"Yes, of course we can," said Olivia.

"Good," Megan whispered. "I'll find a place for the viewing and let you know."

"Absolutely," Olivia answered. "We definitely need to see what you found on the tape."

CHAPTER TWELVE

After the meeting ended, people slowly dribbled out of the room onto the front lawn. Olivia and Wayne stayed back, waiting to hear from Megan about where she would show them the surveillance video she'd found. In a few moments, Megan texted directions to a house not far away from where they were.

"Megan doesn't dare show us the tape here at her home," Olivia remarked as they quickly caught a cab to meet her at the designated location. "The walls at her place could have eyes, she doesn't know who's watching her."

"It's a smart move," Wayne couldn't help but agree. "This tape could be a big boon for her! Just what she's been waiting for. She's being careful about it."

"Interesting that Clay found it, isn't it?" remarked Olivia.

"I was just thinking that," said Wayne, as the cab drove to the location Megan had indicated. "Clay certainly seems to be a strong supporter of Megan's."

*

Olivia and Wayne arrived at an unpretentious home on a small street in Naples and rang the bell.

"No one's here," Megan announced immediately after she opened the door and they entered. "We're completely safe."

It was clear to see the level of apprehension Megan lived under constantly. She didn't feel safe anywhere these days. Could that be a sign of her guilt? Olivia wondered. What was it she feared was going to be found out about her? Waves of distrust of Megan washed over Olivia from time to time. Was Olivia on the wrong track? Could it be that Megan was indeed guilty? Olivia wasn't eliminating that possibility, just keeping it on the back burner so she could be open to whatever else might come along.

Olivia and Wayne followed Megan to a closed porch at the side of the house.

"A friend of mine lives here," Megan offered as they looked around. "She's an old, good friend and offered me the chance to show you the video in her home."

“That’s good of her,” said Olivia. “I’d like to meet your friend soon.”

“When the time is right,” Megan replied once again as she pulled the blinds closed tight and began to run the surveillance video.

In a few moments the film opened with a picture of Tyron sitting on the patio, looking out at the sky. It was startling to see him alive. He looked much more frail than Olivia had imagined. Behind Tyron stood Bella. As the sound on the video got louder, you could hear her screaming at him for all she was worth.

“Listen to me, you idiot!” Bella thundered, giving Olivia chills.

Tyron made no response. Olivia wondered why. It disturbed her.

“I said you have to eat your dinner now.” Bella’s voice was filled with growing rage. “You can’t wait for later. Eat now, you old fool.”

Tyron grimaced, but still did not respond.

“If you don’t listen to me, you’re in trouble.” Bella seemed beside herself. “You eat when I tell you. You wash when it’s time!”

Olivia felt sick to her stomach watching. “This is horrible,” she murmured.

“Does Bella get physical with him?” Wayne interrupted, becoming more distressed.

“She comes just this close of whacking Tyron on the side of the face,” Megan replied as Bella continued to hurl one insult after another at the figure who simply sat immobile, tapping his fingers on the edge of his wheelchair, an air of hopelessness surrounding him.

“Why didn’t Tyron fire Bella instantly?” Olivia asked, breathless.

“That’s a great question!” Megan fired back as the video suddenly ended and she pulled up the blinds. “I asked him that myself, over and over. He wouldn’t answer, though. Tyron clammed up whenever it suited him. I asked if he enjoyed being yelled at. Was he a masochist of some kind? Of course he said nothing.”

“He was shamed, totally shamed,” Wayne uttered.

Olivia suddenly became angry with Megan. “You knew this was going on all the time?” It was hard to believe Megan allowed this.

“In a way.” Megan backtracked a bit. “I could hear Bella’s voice getting louder and louder down there on the patio, but I didn’t always hear exactly what she said.”

"Why didn't you go down and stop it?" Olivia was suspicious. If Megan knew about this and did nothing, she was definitely complicit in what went on.

"I couldn't stop it!" Megan's voice rose. "There was no way."

"Why not?" Why didn't you fire Bella?" Wayne jumped in.

"I wanted to. Believe me, I tried to get him to dump her," Megan spoke swiftly. "I kept telling Tyron we had to get rid of Bella and find him someone new. He yelled back at me that he didn't want to. He wouldn't hear of it. He said I should shut up, that I was causing him pain."

"You were causing him pain? How about Bella?" Olivia couldn't follow any of this.

"Tyron was attached to Bella, he was used to her!" Megan's voice rose.

"How about you? You were his wife! Wasn't he attached to you?" Olivia stood up to Megan.

"It was too scary for him to be without Bella!" Megan yelled at Olivia now. "She was the one he depended on for everything, not me!"

"Wait a minute," Wayne interjected. "Did Bella have something on your husband? Do you happen to know what it was?"

"Bella might have had something on Tyron," Megan murmured, pleased by the idea. "But if she did, I have no idea what it was."

"How could you not know?" Wayne confronted Megan fully.

"Maybe it's better to say I didn't care!" Megan snapped. "Tyron could be rough at times, he'd totally shut you out. In the last few months I meant nothing to him, became just a sideshow. There was no way I could get through to him even if I wanted to. And to tell the truth, seeing him sit out there day after day staring at the sky became unnerving. I was exhausted by him, totally exhausted."

Olivia realized they were only touching the tip of the iceberg about the truth of Megan's marriage. It seemed they all were hiding something, that it was dangerous to reveal the truth.

"Tell me more about your marriage to Tyron," Olivia insisted, looking into Megan's eyes.

"What do you want to hear?"

"The truth," Olivia demanded.

"I told you it was good in the beginning," Megan started and then grew silent.

"And then?" Olivia wasn't letting go.

"We had our differences," Megan said finally.

"A huge age difference for starters," Wayne commented.

"That was the least of it." Megan suddenly grew teary, surprising Olivia. "It's not what everyone thinks, not at all. As the years went by Tyron grew tired of me."

"The way he grew tired of Alice?" Olivia murmured.

"Maybe?" Megan liked that idea. "Tyron needed something fresh, new, and glittery all the time. He got bored, he got restless. He constantly demanded that the people around him make him feel good."

"I can see how that could be exhausting," Olivia murmured.

Grateful for the acknowledgment, Megan continued. "I always had to dress up for him, surprise him. It became my job to make him laugh and feel young again. But when things didn't go well and he became gloomy, no matter what I tried, there was nothing I could do. He'd tell me things weren't working. He'd say it over and over again."

"That had to be unnerving," said Olivia, grimly. "You must have grown to hate him?"

Megan looked at Olivia strangely. "Hate him? No. But you're right, it was incredibly unnerving at times!"

Olivia felt a strange chill go through her as Megan spoke. She had the sense of Megan as almost being helpless at Tyron's side. "I'm sorry," said Olivia.

"Thank you," Megan uttered. "I needed to hear somebody say that to me."

Olivia felt a strange bond with Megan then, feeling once again how lost Megan had been and probably still was.

"Naturally I pulled away a bit," Megan continued, "and it really didn't matter because Tyron had grown totally dependent on Bella by then."

"Which is why there was no way he'd ever fire her," Olivia added.

"Of course not." Megan's eyes lit up. "Tyron was obviously scared to death to lose her and start with someone new. Who knew what would happen then? The horror you know is better than the horror that's coming, isn't it?"

Megan's analysis of the situation made sense to Olivia. "People who are vulnerable and dependent often experience abuse at the hands of their caretakers," Olivia remarked.

"Yes, they do." Megan seemed quite aware of that. "And they dish it out too, don't forget about that. They get back at others in weird ways."

Wayne wasn't buying this. He suddenly intervened. "Bella's yelling at Tyron didn't disturb you, though? You didn't want to protect your husband?" Wayne couldn't seem to get beyond that point.

"I never said it didn't disturb me, did I?" Megan grew rattled. "But as Tyron got sicker, there was only so much power I had with him. I told you. He needed help all the time."

"And you couldn't be the one to give it to him," Olivia echoed.

"Of course I couldn't. Could you?" Megan's eyes flashed. "It all became too much to handle."

"You must have wanted to get out of the marriage badly then, didn't you?" Wayne started probing deeper.

Megan suddenly looked wounded. "Not necessarily," she replied. "I cared for Tyron, I wished him well. We had good times together before he got sick. Even after he got sick, in the beginning, things were okay."

Olivia listened closely, but Megan's voice had now become flat. Talking to Wayne, it seemed she started repeating the same party line over and over. How could any young woman not feel trapped in a situation like this, though?

"Are you coming to the funeral tomorrow morning?" Megan changed the topic of conversation swiftly then.

"Yes, we are," Olivia responded.

"Good, you'll hear them all speak about Tyron. Don't believe anything you hear. They're just putting on a show. Deep down they're all vultures."

"We're prepared for everything," Wayne replied.

"And what do you think about the video I have here?" Megan returned to the main point. "Is this solid evidence against Bella?" Megan seemed intent upon defending herself.

"I don't know if the video is solid evidence," Wayne answered slowly. "But it doesn't look good for Bella now. At the very least, it raises suspicion."

"We'll talk to Bella again after the funeral," Olivia added. "Can we tell her about the video?"

"Yes, you can!" Megan's eyes flashed. "See how she defends herself once she hears you have something on her. And show the video to the police as well. This should take their focus off me, shouldn't it?"

"Maybe yes, maybe no," Olivia answered, suddenly sad. "The video is circumstantial, but it should certainly cause the police to broaden their view and think twice about Bella."

Megan flipped her head back and shook her hair off her shoulders. "Well, it's better than nothing! I'll see you at the funeral tomorrow."

"Yes," said Wayne, "and directly after that, we'll talk to Bella."

"What are you going to do in the meantime?" Megan zeroed in on Wayne, wanting an accounting of their activities.

"I'm investigating Tyron's finances and business dealings," Wayne reported. "Olivia's spending her time talking to the different people involved in his life."

"Like who?" Megan's eyes flashed.

"Like Alice, Kayle, Lana, and others," Olivia answered, wanting to be circumspect. "Even though she was technically working for Megan she wanted the freedom to talk to whoever caught her eye. Olivia wondered if she should ask for permission to speak to Megan's friends and acquaintances now. If she did, she was concerned that Megan might feel that she was under investigation herself.

"Do you have any other suggestions for me?" Olivia asked.

"Of course I have," Megan said softly. "But the time has to be right. First I want to see how things go. And what's your guess now? Who do you think did it?" Megan challenged Olivia, seeking reassurance that Olivia didn't suspect her.

"I truly don't know yet," Olivia said truthfully.

"But who do you suspect?" Megan zeroed in.

"I'm always careful not to suspect anyone until I have solid evidence," Olivia responded.

"And what if you never get any solid evidence?" Megan wouldn't back down.

"I always do," Olivia replied. "If I'm patient enough and thorough enough and go step by step with my eyes wide open, the truth is always revealed."

Megan seemed startled. "Always?"

"It never fails," said Olivia firmly. "The truth has a life of its own. It can only be hidden for so long."

Megan spun away then. "I'll see you both at the funeral," she repeated as she quickly went out the door.

*

The funeral was being held in an old stone church in Naples, not far from the very end of town. Even though it was early in the morning, the place was filled to overflowing. Olivia was surprised to see how many had turned out for the final good-bye to Tyron. She and Wayne slipped into a pew in the back row and looked around.

"Did Tyron really have this many friends?" Olivia asked.

"Nobody wants to miss out on this event." Wayne looked around. "There are business acquaintances here, friends, old-timers he knew. But it's the way he died that's drawing everybody. And, for all we know, the killer's right here in our midst."

Olivia shivered. "Who? Point them out to me."

Wayne shook his head. "Not sure yet. Just sensing it out carefully."

"Did you find something about Tyron's business dealings that makes you say that?" Olivia asked.

"His dealings were convoluted and lots of people were on the take," Wayne reported. "Tyron invested in questionable business deals too. He probably raked in more money than he should have. But he gave a lot away to charity, too. A lot of the charities he gave to must be seated right here, too."

"Did what he gave to others and received for himself balance out?" asked Olivia.

"In a way it did," Wayne replied. "But there's definitely the possibility that someone didn't get what they thought was their due. This could be a vengeance killing. "

"Could be," Olivia murmured, "but I don't think so. Tyron would have had to have done something truly awful to someone to be killed the way he was. That's not the feel I have of him."

"No, it's not," Wayne agreed. "Of course, Bella could have had enough and in the heat of the moment, given him a good shove. She seemed pretty irate in the video. It could have been something that happened on impulse."

"No, that's not it." Olivia didn't agree. "There's no residual evidence of any kind. It couldn't be an impulse killing, seems too carefully planned out."

Suddenly the church chimes rang out and the pastor stood in front of the crowd. To begin he offered a prayer and then hymns. The organ played and the congregation joined in the singing. The grim mood in the church began to lift as it filled with song.

"We have come here to honor our beloved father, husband, friend, and companion of many years," the pastor started. "There are many who wish to stand up and speak about Tyron. First, I will call up his dear daughter, Kayle."

Kayle, walking pointedly, went up to the center of the platform, took the microphone, and without any hesitation began speaking about her beloved father. She started by saying how the loss of him would haunt her the rest of her life.

"Why didn't they start the eulogies with Megan?" Olivia asked. "After all, she's the wife."

"I doubt that Megan will get up in front of the crowd and speak," Wayne replied. "She feels too threatened and disliked. It was probably all she could do to show up."

Olivia looked around the church then to see if she could spot Megan. She finally saw her sitting at the edge of a front row with two young women beside her.

"Those young women must be some of the friends she was talking about," Olivia whispered to Wayne.

"Must be." Wayne seemed strangely unconcerned about Megan though.

Olivia looked to see if Cameron Fern was around somewhere as well. So far, she didn't see her.

After Kayle completed her eulogy, Lana came up and said a few words. She emphasized how her father's long illness had ruined not only his life but his judgment. And how hard it had been for everyone. That was a subtle barb at Megan, thought Olivia. Lana was obviously pointing to his judgment about marrying her—even though he hadn't gotten ill until *after* marrying Megan.

After that, to everyone's surprise, Tyron's ex-wife , Alice, was called to the platform. Dressed in a black silk dress with a black lace veil on her head, she was clearly playing the role of the grieving widow.

"I feel compelled to publicly say good-bye to Tyron," Alice spoke in a strange and broken tone. "Despite the seeming rupture in our relationship, we stayed close over all the years. And now this horrible parting. I'm here to say I'm sorry, I'm here to say this is wrong. Tyron didn't deserve this. I didn't either."

The church grew silent as she spoke.

"It's brave of her to speak here," Wayne commented.

Olivia didn't agree and she didn't like it. Olivia felt strangely disturbed as Alice went on and on.

"I don't think it's so brave," Olivia replied. "It's Megan who should be up there speaking. But Alice probably intimidated her."

"There's no reason to think that." Wayne looked perplexed.

"Megan is much younger than Alice. She stole away her husband and now that Tyron's gone, the two of them are vying for position," said Olivia. "Look at Megan over there."

Megan seemed practically crumpled in her seat in the corner. Oddly, Clay was sitting behind her, his hand on Megan's shoulder now.

"Clay seems to feel bad for Megan, doesn't he?" Olivia continued.

"Seems like Clay's trying to give her strength," Wayne commented, standing up and looking over at him.

"It seems like he's a decent guy," said Olivia, "the only one of them who cares about her at all."

"Yes, it does," Wayne agreed, "and I can see why. They're in similar positions in a way, both married to much older spouses. Clay relates to Megan's situation. They probably have a lot in common."

"They do have a lot in common," Olivia replied. "They're both trapped in this crazy family."

"Megan and Clay's connection raises questions, though, wouldn't you say?" asked Wayne.

Olivia had just been wondering about it as well. "It could, of course," she murmured. "I could see how it could have disturbed Alice, if she realized."

"Of course she realized. She realizes everything," Wayne quipped as Alice's voice rang out loudly in the church.

"Tyron was my beloved once and always." Alice went on and on. "He was a good man, he had a good heart, but he got trapped by all kinds of people."

"Just listen to Alice going on and on," said Olivia. "It sounds like she's coming apart at the seams."

"She probably always was that way," said Wayne.

"So, I could see why Clay would want to be close to someone his age," Olivia commented. "What kind of marriage could it be for Clay?"

"It's a marriage he chose," Wayne said slowly. "You don't know why he chose it either, and neither do I."

CHAPTER THIRTEEN

Just before the funeral ended, Olivia and Wayne slipped out and stood to the side of the church. Olivia was waiting to see what would happen next. In a little while, the church doors opened and the people streamed out onto the street. Before long the sidewalk in front of the church was overflowing.

Olivia looked around carefully to see who had attended and where they were now. Most had come with others but a few were here alone. Bella stood by herself on the sidelines, watching everybody, and Megan left her two friends and rushed home immediately.

Alice and Clay, Kayle and her fiancé, and Lana stood at the center of the gathering accepting condolences. Others gathered together in small clusters to talk before dispersing and leaving their dear friend Tyron behind.

Olivia and Wayne edged over to Bella slowly and stood beside her for a few moments.

"A terrible day, isn't it?" Olivia remarked.

"A tragic day," Bella muttered, not meeting Olivia's eyes.

"Please accept our condolences," Wayne offered.

"Thank you very much," said Bella. "Not one other person here has said that to me. No one even noticed I was attending. In their eyes, I'm nothing, but I was the one who took care of him day after day, night after night. I'm the only one who's really grieving."

"You did a fine job," Wayne interjected.

"Maybe." Bella shrugged. "But did you hear all the stuff they said in there about him? It was all a show. None of it meant a thing. Not one of them really gave a damn."

"Megan didn't give a damn?" asked Wayne.

Bella shrugged and looked around. "Megan gave such a damn she didn't say a word at the funeral and just ran away as fast as she could."

Bella was being harsh, thought Olivia. There were many reasons that Megan might not have been able to speak and had to get away.

"Do you think we could have a little time with you back home today?" Olivia asked quickly.

"Why?" Bella seemed surprised by the request.

"We just want to talk to you a bit more before you leave the home," Wayne explained.

Bella bristled. "Who said I'm leaving? I'm not leaving the home so fast. The police want me to stay there until they've gotten all the information they need."

"They have a lot of it already," Wayne replied. "It won't take much longer."

"Who knows?" Bella objected.

"The police are hoping you can help them," Olivia said, "and we're hoping you can help us too."

Bella seemed to like that. It must have made her feel important. "Okay," she answered. "Come over anytime. Come over now. In fact, the sooner the better."

As Olivia and Wayne accompanied Bella back to the home a silence fell over all of them in the cab.

"I miss the old guy," Bella said as the taxi pulled up to the door. "This shouldn't have happened. Tyron died before his time and everyone knows it."

Olivia felt bad for Bella. "Where will you go after this is all over?"

Bella tipped her head and looked at Olivia strangely. "It's never gonna be over," she muttered. "If you ask me, it's gonna go on and on for years. The court cases are gonna wind all over each other and trip each other up. And the family is going to want me to stay on right where I am, because they'll all need me on their side. Everyone knows that I was the one who was there from the beginning. I'm the one who remembers everything."

Olivia was startled by Bella's response. "You remember everything?"

"I have a memory like an elephant. I never forget. Nothing slips my mind. I remember what went on every single day," Bella continued.

"And you've told law enforcement all that you know?" Wayne jumped in immediately.

"When someone asks a question, I answer," Bella remarked. "I don't know what they need to know until they ask me, do I?"

The three of them got out of the taxi and went into the house. Their steps echoed on the floor of the entranceway and the place seemed empty and forlorn.

"It's crazy to be at the house without him," Bella said sadly then.

"Where is everybody?" asked Wayne.

"They're all going out to eat after the funeral," Bella remarked. "No one will be back here for a few hours, thank God. You can ask me what you want in peace. I won't have to look over my shoulder."

"How about Megan?" Olivia asked. "Where did she go? Isn't she here somewhere?"

Bella shrugged. "Megan has hardly said two words to me since Tyron died. She's probably hiding away upstairs in her quarters. Or maybe she's with her friends. How do I know?"

"Is she different from the way she was before?" Wayne needed to know.

"In the beginning Megan was around a lot of the time," Bella replied. "As time went on, I saw her less and less. This past month or so she's been like a shadow, drifting in and out. A strange shadow, I'd say."

Olivia took it all in. Clearly, Bella was insinuating something about Megan. Olivia wanted to get the whole story quickly, but didn't want to scare Bella off.

"Let's go sit in the main room and talk," Wayne suggested.

Bella agreed to it immediately and they all went in and sat down. The main room was large and quiet now, except for the sound of the wind blowing outside.

"Rain's coming later tonight," Bella murmured. "Tyron loved it when it rained. He'd sit at the window in here and watch the rain fall for hours."

The image was haunting. "What was he thinking about?" asked Olivia. "Was he a lonely man?"

Bella smirked. "Funny that you say that. Everyone thinks Tyron had the whole world at his fingertips, but you're absolutely right. Basically, he had no one, he was extremely lonely. Whoever he had was around for his money. And he wasn't stupid, he realized that."

Olivia wondered if that also included Bella, but she didn't say anything.

"Tyron was lonely even though he was married to Megan?" Wayne abruptly joined the conversation. "Was he lonely even during the early part of their marriage?"

"The early part was the early part." Bella ran her hand over her arms. "Everyone's happy in the beginning, aren't they?"

Olivia flinched at the comment. Bella had an odd wisdom of her own.

"I heard Tyron was completely infatuated with Megan when they met," Olivia commented.

"Yes, that's right, he was." Bella gazed away. "Believe it or not, I actually tried to warn him about her then. I said, she's not as pretty as you think, honey. Tyron looked at me funny and paid no attention. Then I said, a pretty face doesn't last very long. In a way I saw what was coming. I didn't see him killed this way, though."

Rankled, Olivia stood up from the sofa. In her own meek way, Bella was powerful and also frightening. Olivia couldn't get the video of Bella screaming at Tyron out of her mind.

"How did you see Tyron's life going?" Olivia asked quickly.

"I didn't think about it much, actually." Bella stood up too then. "And I didn't have to wonder either. Tyron actually told me how he felt about most things. I became his confidant as the years went by. Who else could he really talk to? Who else would listen to him and not make a fuss? Tyron trusted me."

"That's good," said Olivia, encouraging Bella to continue.

Bella smiled and nodded. "It was good that he could talk to me, for sure. Tyron got more and more upset with Megan over time. How couldn't he? Things didn't stay as they were."

"They never do," murmured Wayne.

"Megan's true colors started to come out," Bella continued. "She really couldn't stand Tyron, and anyone with half a brain could see that. Including Tyron. But he was too ashamed to admit he'd made a mistake and that he couldn't stand her. After all, he had a young beautiful wife and it made him look good in everyone's eyes. People looked up to him and he wasn't about to spoil that."

"What about his ex-wife, Alice?" Olivia asked quickly.

"What about her?" Bella's lip curled. "She wanted him back badly, never left him alone."

"That must have upset Megan, didn't it?" Olivia asked.

"Of course it upset Megan, and I think Tyron loved that. He enjoyed the power of having the two women battling over him. And he kept the whole thing going. He let Alice keep coming and begging him to return. Then he'd tell Megan about it."

"That's lousy," said Olivia.

Bella grinned. "Tyron did it to get back at Megan. Deep down he was pissed with himself for getting caught in her snare. He'd made a fool of himself and he knew it. But Megan was smart, she still had power over him. And it gave her pleasure to use it. She'd look at magazines of handsome male models and ooh and ahh about them in front of Tyron."

"Disgusting," Wayne spit out.

"It was disgusting." Bella laughed. "Tyron didn't take it lightly either. The more she did it, the sicker he started to feel. Do you want the truth?" Bella suddenly spun around and crouched down.

"Of course I do." Olivia was frightened.

"Recently, Tyron began telling me he really had enough and wanted to get away from Megan. I told him I could understand why. I even encouraged him to do it. What the hell do you need the bitch for, I said to him."

"Oh my." Olivia felt something awful coming.

"And then one day, not long ago, Tyron really had enough. He actually begged me to get rid of Megan for him." Bella looked relieved to be speaking about this. "I was frightened at first when he said that. Then I thought his mind might be going."

"What did he mean by get rid of her, exactly?" Wayne now looked alarmed. "To kill Megan?"

"Tyron just said get that woman out of my life, Bella! Get her out of my home!" Bella's voice became raspy. "Tyron definitely didn't want Megan around. The truth is she became rougher and rougher on him when she found out he was using escorts."

"Wait a minute, back up!" Olivia held up her hand. "Did you say Tyron was using escorts?"

"Routinely." Bella sneered again. "An old guy like that! But he needed them. He was lonely, as you say."

"The escorts came here to the house?" Olivia was appalled.

"They sure did," said Bella. "Tyron made no bones about it either. When Megan found out, she was furious at first. She said he was making a fool of her in front of everyone. It didn't bother Tyron at all, though. He had a secret arrangement with the escorts and their service, but everybody knew what was going on. I think he wanted it that way, too."

"He wanted everyone to know he was cheating on Megan?" Olivia felt sick inside.

"Yes, that's right. It gave him a feeling of power. Go ask his daughters! Kayle and Lana will back me up. Go talk to Megan's friend Andrea, too. I'm sure Megan told her about it."

Olivia looked away. This was a den of snakes they'd stepped into.

Bella went on, triumphantly now. "I'm not lying, I'm telling the truth. And things got so bad recently that Tyron actually offered me money to get rid of Megan."

"Wait a minute!" Wayne was stone-faced now. "You're saying Tyron actually offered you money to make Megan disappear?"

"Yes," Bella burst out. "And he did it a few days before he suddenly died! Megan might have found out, right?"

Bella's words fell like stones into the middle of the room.

"Do you have proof of this, Bella?" Wayne immediately asked. "We need solid proof."

"I have no written proof," Bella replied. "But I think Tyron made the same offer to some of the escorts."

"To give them money to have Megan disappear?" Wayne's face had grown pale.

"Something like that," Bella whispered. "I'm not positive, I'm not sure. But it backfired anyway, didn't it?"

"Could one of the escorts have arranged to have him killed?" Olivia was horrified. "Could she have been a friend of Megan's?"

"I doubt it," Bella hissed. "Who would risk their life to save Megan? My guess is that the killer had to be someone who hated Tyron and was sick and tired of his being around."

Once again Bella was pointing the finger at Megan, thought Olivia. Then she remembered the video of Bella screaming at Tyron. Megan had given it to them, pointing the finger at Bella. Olivia decided to explore Bella's part in all this immediately.

"We have a surveillance video of you and Tyron," Olivia interrupted sharply, wondering how Bella would respond.

Bella seemed unconcerned.

"The video shows you screaming at Tyron, abusing him," Olivia continued. "Seems like you couldn't stand having him around anymore either!"

"That's not true," Bella claimed. "Sure, I got pissed at Tyron from time to time because he could be a brat. But I wasn't abusing him at all. I was trying to get him to do what he had to. He could be rough to handle! Everyone knows that. And it was my job to make sure he did what he had to do. It was up to me to keep him well."

Bella's unruffled manner surprised Olivia.

"Who gave you the video, anyway?" Bella asked then, lightly smiling. "I bet it was Megan, right?"

Olivia wasn't sure if she should tell Bella.

"Who else do you think might have found the video?" Wayne was trying to corner Bella as well.

Bella almost took the bait and then pulled back. "It doesn't matter who," she said finally. "They're all a bunch of loonies. So I yelled at the guy to make him listen. It doesn't amount to anything!"

Wayne's phone rang suddenly then, breaking into the intensity between them. Wayne went to the table to pick it up and Olivia turned to watch him. To her surprise, as she did so, she saw the door to the room they were in barely open. Then she saw someone peeking in.

"Who's there?" Olivia asked, rushing to the door as the figure disappeared quickly.

"That had to be Megan," Bella exclaimed. "I told you, she's become a ghost these days! She does that a lot, peeks in through doors and windows and then runs away."

"Megan, Megan," Olivia called out to her as she ran through the door herself, to find who had been there. No one could be seen at all, though.

Olivia quickly ran through the rooms and then up the stairs, looking for the figure who'd been looking in.

"Megan," Olivia called, as she opened one door after another, going into a room and then out again. Megan was nowhere to be found, nor was anybody else. Whoever had been inside had most likely left the home immediately.

Unnerved, Olivia returned to the main room, where Bella and Wayne were still waiting.

"I couldn't find anybody at all," breathed Olivia.

Bella shrugged and smiled. "It doesn't surprise me at all. I told you, she's like a ghost, recently. Appearing and disappearing like that. Megan has her ways and places she hides in."

"This has been going on for a while?" Olivia double-checked.

"Yes, it has." Bella smirked now.

"Megan must be terrified," Olivia remarked.

"Who cares?" sneered Bella. "If she's terrified, that's a sign of her guilt, isn't it?"

"Seems so," Wayne agreed softly.

"Not necessarily," Olivia countered. "It's a sign that she's being threatened, that's all. Who knows by whom, exactly?" Then Olivia turned to Bella. "Maybe Megan found out that Tyron offered you money to make her disappear."

"Maybe she did," said Bella glumly. "So what?"

"That could terrify anyone, couldn't it? Maybe Megan's afraid of you? Checking up to see what you're up to?"

At that Bella guffawed loudly. "A thousand maybes don't add up to anything, though, do they? She's not the one who was killed! It was Tyron."

Wayne walked over to Olivia then. "Bella's right. So far, this is all just speculation," he said. "When you were looking for Megan, I was talking to the police over the phone. They want us over at the station as soon as possible for a meeting. The district attorney will be there and wants to go over new evidence they've found."

"Good!" Bella barked. "Go hear the evidence against her!"

"Let's go and hear what new evidence they found," Olivia replied.

"And when you find out, give a call and let me know." Bella looked excited.

"Whatever we hear will be confidential," Wayne replied.

"Yeah, yeah, confidential," said Bella. "Everything's confidential, until it's not."

CHAPTER FOURTEEN

Olivia was relieved to get out of the house and be on the way to the police station with Wayne. She felt uncomfortable spending time with Bella and was greatly disturbed to hear about Tyron's involvement with escorts. Also, the odd experience of seeing someone peering in through the door had been unnerving. If it was Megan, as Olivia suspected, it might mean that she was coming apart. The fear and horror Megan was experiencing might be too much for her. That didn't make her a murderer, though. Olivia refused to jump to that conclusion.

"Do you think it's true that Tyron used escorts regularly?" Olivia asked Wayne as the cab rolled through the elegant streets of Naples where everything was glittering and in perfect order.

"I can't imagine Bella would lie about something like that," Wayne replied. "It's easy to check up on it, anyway."

"We have to check it out right away," said Olivia.

"We certainly do," Wayne agreed.

"I can see how something like that could drive Megan completely crazy," Olivia breathed. "It had to feel like a huge slap in her face."

"It's not as unusual as you might imagine, though," said Wayne, trying to normalize the situation. "Lots of guys get hooked on escorts, including older ones."

Olivia knew she had to accept that reality, even though she found it distasteful. "But what else does that tell us about Tyron?"

"It doesn't say anything much about Tyron, but of course it puts his marriage in a bad light," Wayne commented. "And it certainly could speak to motive for Megan. When exactly did she find out about these escorts? How long had it been going on? That's very important."

"A jury could relate to her upset, I believe," Olivia murmured.

"Maybe. It depends who they are," said Wayne staunchly. "But if Megan's now taking it upon herself to peer through doors, that makes her seem even more desperate. Who knows what else she might have overheard Tyron saying? If she found out he wanted her gone, it makes sense that she would have decided to get rid of him before he got to her."

"Self-defense?" mused Olivia.

"There are better ways of defending yourself." Wayne didn't like it. "It sounds as though they had a weird power struggle going on for some time."

Olivia felt a case building against Megan from every corner, one insinuation at a time. All put together, it could do her in. It almost felt like a tidal wave was growing against Megan that would be almost impossible to overcome. Olivia didn't like it. The situation was too complex to stop searching.

"What about Bella?" Olivia remarked. "How reliable is she? Are we just brushing off her video because she makes light of it?"

"Who says we're brushing it off? I made sure the police got a copy. I don't see any motive with Bella, frankly," said Wayne. "It's natural for caretakers to get frustrated and cranky. I'm sure lots of them lose their tempers at times."

Wayne was downplaying Bella's possible involvement. He clearly didn't feel good about Megan, or anything about her.

"We have to stay neutral here," Olivia warned him as their cab quickly approached the station. "No matter how strange Megan now seems, we have to keep our minds open."

"My mind is always open," Wayne replied as the cab stopped and he got out and paid.

*

When Olivia and Wayne walked into the conference room at the police station everyone was already there. They all stood up as Olivia and Wayne entered, including James Gallant, Marcus Brandt, and Ed Mahoney. Olivia felt pleased, happy to be part of a team.

"This is Marvin Toll, our district attorney." James introduced Olivia and Wayne to a tall, angular man with deep creases between his brow and a shock of dark hair over his forehead.

"Pleased to meet you," Olivia and Wayne responded as they all sat down to start the meeting.

"We asked you to join us as soon as you could because we have important new evidence," James Gallant said. "Firstly, we spoke to Aldo Gapa, who runs a prominent charity in town. Tyron was a big donor to his charity and Aldo told us that recently Megan tried to stop Tyron from contributing. It definitely raised alarm bells for them."

"Why would she do that?" Olivia was startled.

"That's the question, isn't it?" said Gallant. "At the very least, Megan was definitely trying to take control of how Tyron spent his money. Needless to say, her meddling upset Aldo considerably. It also disturbed quite a few other people at the charity as well. Several began questioning what Megan was up to."

"What are you implying?" Wayne asked directly.

Gallant answered immediately. "People wondered why Megan was interfering. She personally had a huge allowance from Tyron and her credit card was always charged to the brim. Tyron took care of her monthly charges, naturally. Not a word said."

"How do you know he didn't say a word about it?" Olivia broke in.

"There was never a late payment and we never heard anything to the contrary," Gallant crisply replied.

Marvin Toll nodded his head forcibly in agreement and joined in. "And beyond that, as we told Wayne over the phone, we have important new evidence as well. I was waiting for us all to be together to make it public."

Olivia sat up taller. "What is it?" she asked directly.

"Megan recently told someone who worked at her company that she planned to move her business very soon to another part of the state."

The room bristled with interest. Things were definitely piling on.

"Why was Megan doing that?" Marvin continued. "Where was she going, exactly? Was she planning to leave Tyron behind? Was she thinking of getting a divorce? Or was it simpler for her to just arrange for him to conveniently die?"

Olivia took a deep, sharp breath. Clearly Megan was becoming the fall guy here. "Who told you this?" she asked.

"I am not at liberty to give you the informant's name, but we definitely have firm evidence," Marvin responded swiftly. "The informant gave us all the paperwork we need to corroborate Megan's plans. The moment the informant heard that Tyron had died, she felt we had to have this. It seems definitely possible that Megan was setting the groundwork not only for the move, but for Tyron's demise."

"Anything else?" Wayne stood up then and confronted Marvin directly.

"Yes, there's more. Sit down," Marvin continued. "Naturally, we've been looking into all of Megan's activities. It also seems that she is still quite involved with friends from her old escort agency."

Megan had told Olivia such, but still, Olivia was startled now that she thought about it. This could have endless implications. She wondered if Megan's old escort agency was the same one that Tyron used presently.

"Tell us whatever you know about Tyron's escorts, please," Marvin addressed Olivia and Wayne then. "Any additional information would be greatly appreciated."

"We just heard that Tyron hired escorts regularly," Olivia replied.

"Who told you?" Marvin was interested.

"We heard it from Bella, Tyron's caretaker," Wayne replied.

James Gallant jumped in. "Did Bella tell you if Megan's friends work for the same agency that provided Tyron his escorts?"

"I have no idea about that," replied Wayne.

"We've all been wondering whether Megan knew Tyron's escorts personally." Gallant was on a roll. "Did one of them visit Tyron the day of his death and follow Megan's orders?"

It was a frightening theory and Olivia shuddered. "You're suggesting that Megan ordered a hit job?" she asked.

"Maybe so," Marvin joined in forcefully. "Given everything we have, there seems to be no doubt, however, about Megan's involvement in Tyron's death."

"It does look possible," Wayne had to agree.

"Therefore," Marvin went on, "I wanted to let you know that I've spoken to Megan's lawyer and urged her to accept a plea deal for her client. She adamantly refused."

"A plea deal?" Olivia was appalled.

"Not only will a plea deal make it much easier for Megan, but it will save the community a great deal of time, expense, and bad publicity," Marvin added. "I'm strongly requesting that you and Wayne urge Megan to reconsider."

"What would Megan be pleading to?" asked Wayne.

"That's something we can work out with her lawyer," Marvin replied.

"Absolutely not!" Olivia interrupted forcefully. "I can't encourage Megan to go along with it. This is totally premature!"

Marvin smiled at Olivia condescendingly. "Not premature at all," he replied. "When you've done as many cases as I have, you can easily see the handwriting on the wall."

"Then it's good that I haven't done as many cases," Olivia retorted, "because all I see are accusations lining up. At the moment they're all just assumptions." Olivia thought of all the other possible suspects who hadn't been fully explored at all, the ex-wife, Alice, who was overly involved with Tyron; Bella, who'd been seen on the video abusing Tyron. And who knew who else?

"There are plenty of other suspects still out there," Olivia insisted.

Marvin threw a strange glance at Olivia. "Really? Like who?"

"I understand you've seen the video of Bella yelling at Tyron?" Olivia asked.

"Yes, we've seen it." Gallant stepped in. "It's definitely troubling, but Bella doesn't have motive to do something so heinous."

"How about the first wife, Alice?" Megan went on.

Gallant shook his head strongly. "There's absolutely no evidence against Alice at all. In fact, she just remarried. She's been out and about a great deal. Her life had grown better."

"You don't know that for sure," Olivia snapped. "Seems Alice's husband, Clay, and Megan have a close relationship."

Marvin wasn't interested. "We can't go there, it doesn't amount to anything. We've checked it out. Alice and Clay have a good relationship. She's part of Clay's group of friends. Alice and Clay often go to Club Seeward together. It's full of younger folks."

Olivia was surprised that they'd checked it so fully. "Megan's relationship with Clay could still be troubling for Alice, couldn't it?" Olivia insisted.

Marvin looked irritated. "It doesn't matter. It's irrelevant," he insisted, before turning to Wayne. "How about you?" he continued. "Do you agree with Olivia? Do you also feel it's a bad idea to encourage Megan to take a plea deal?"

"Actually I do," Wayne said slowly. "I agree that a plea deal is premature. But I also feel that you've gathered a lot of important information. We have to follow the trail and see where it leads. I'll go immediately to speak to the escort service Tyron used and see what they have to tell me."

"Okay, go ahead," Marvin replied haughtily, "but we don't want to keep this case in the spotlight forever. And remember, the offer of a plea deal won't last forever either."

*

Once out on the street Olivia couldn't settle down for a moment. "They're ganging up on Megan from every angle," she breathed.

"They have just cause for being concerned." Wayne tried to calm Olivia.

"I don't see just cause," Olivia answered.

"Because you're too involved," Wayne breathed. "Even though Megan hired us, and we're working for her, if you look from their perspective, there is just cause."

"There are plenty other people who seek to gain a great deal from Tyron's death as well," said Olivia.

"Yes, there are," Wayne slowly agreed. "But first we have to dispel the suspicions that are directed at Megan. I'll go to the escort service and find out more. Did they know Megan? Was she involved with the women who visited Tyron?"

"You go," Olivia agreed, "and I'll talk to Megan's close friends. She can't be a total monster. We need to see all sides of the picture."

"We certainly do," Wayne agreed.

Wayne left to speak to the escort service. Olivia chose to spend a little while alone before visiting with Andrea, the friend of Megan's that Bella mentioned.

*

Rather than call Andrea immediately, Olivia decided to take some time to herself down at the beach to sort everything out. To Olivia's delight it was high tide when she arrived and the sand was practically empty. It was wonderful to watch the waves breaking loudly, splashing up against the jetties.

Olivia took off her shoes and walked barefoot over the sand to the large rocks and climbed onto one of them easily. She let the sounds of the ocean and salty fresh air soothe and cleanse her. Being a detective was more grueling than she'd imagined, even with a wonderful partner like Wayne. Every day Olivia faced what could turn into a life-and-death decision. Every day she had to unravel layers of lies, innuendos, and deceit. How had she gotten herself into this position? she wondered, as a large seagull swooped down and perched on the jetty beside her.

Olivia turned to the seagull and smiled. He was big, proud, and seemed perfectly content to be sitting here beside her. How simple the seagull's life seemed, without a care in the world. How content he was just to be planted on a beautiful rock. For a moment Olivia longed to return to a life of simplicity and ease. Suddenly she wished she'd never met Todd, or had to go through the horror of his murder. That had been the start of a chain of events that had taken her into a totally different world. It was as if an undertow that she'd had no control over had gripped her, whirled her around, and landed her in an underworld she couldn't get out of. The undertow had actually brought her here now, trying to understand why someone had wanted to throw an old man in a wheelchair down a flight of stairs to his sudden death.

Olivia breathed the wonderful, salty air deeply as a huge wave whirled in front of her. It reminded her of the great force that made high tide and low tide, arranged all things in its own way. As the wind blew up, the seagull suddenly flew away , leaving Olivia perched on the rock alone. She sat there hoping for the wisdom and guidance to know how to protect those who were innocent and help bring to justice those who were sources of harm.

CHAPTER FIFTEEN

After Olivia left, Wayne headed straight to the escort service that had serviced Tyron. Not surprisingly it was located down near the clubs and pier in a small building covered with a large awning. The police had found out which agency Tyron had used and had put in a call letting the owner, Salty Radding, know Wayne was on the way. It seemed Salty offered no objection or seemed in the least bit nonplussed.

When Wayne arrived, Salty greeted him immediately and welcomed him into the back room. Salty was a gruff, stocky good-looking guy in his early fifties. With thick dark hair and somewhat unshaven, he seemed ready for whatever life had to throw at him.

"Nice to meet you." Salty extended a big hand.

"Thanks for seeing me on such short notice." Wayne looked around at the dimly lit surroundings.

"Okay, let me have it. Hold nothing back," Salty started. "Nobody here was happy when they heard about what happened to Tyron."

Wayne realized that this entire agency must have known him very well. "What happened to him, Salty?" Wayne decided to start in a low-key manner.

"Your guess is as good as mine, isn't it?" Salty rubbed his face. "All I can tell you is Tyron was a good customer for a long time. He was good to the girls and they were good to him, too."

Wayne wondered if that was unusual. "Tyron had lots of different escorts? There was no one special?" he asked.

"Every one of our girls is special," Salty countered, grinning. "And Tyron liked variety. He liked them all. We had lots of different women visiting his home and taking care of him, if you know what I mean?"

Wayne nodded. Seemed this was an open secret and no one was trying to keep it under wraps. "Tyron didn't tell you guys to keep it secret?" Wayne asked just to be certain.

Salty laughed. "This isn't exactly the crime of the century, is it?" he asked.

Wayne smiled along with him.

"Didn't seem as if he were covering it up," Salty went on. "Some of our customers do, of course. They're scared someone will find out. Tyron wasn't. His wife, Megan, knew all about it."

Wayne lurched forward in his chair. "How long did Megan know about it? How long had it been going on?" he asked intently.

Salty shrugged and grimaced. "It was a couple of years at least. It wasn't a big deal."

"So it definitely wasn't something recent," Wayne murmured.

"Heck, no," Salty said. "Why? You think Megan just found out?"

"That's crossed our minds," Wayne responded as Salty shook his head.

"We also wondered if this was the agency Megan worked for when she was in the business?" Wayne plunged ahead.

"No, it wasn't," said Salty solemnly. "We have quite a few escort services in Florida. This wasn't hers."

"She doesn't have friends in this service?" Wayne zeroed in.

"Not that I know of," Salty assured him.

That information was good for Megan, thought Wayne. It made her seem less implicated.

"How did Megan feel about what was going on?" Wayne continued, needing to understand this completely.

"If you asked me, it was a relief for her," said Salty confidentially. "Lots of times it's a big relief for the wives, though few of them will admit it. Basically, Megan hated Tyron, she couldn't stand the guy."

Wayne perked up. "What makes you say that?"

"Everyone knew that, it was common knowledge." Salty's voice dropped. "When a guy starts calling for girls all the time, it not only means the marriage is over. It means the guy's lonely, going crazy on his own."

"Tyron called for girls all the time?" asked Wayne.

"Yeah," Salty went on. "No one was surprised about it either."

"Why did Megan hate him so much?" Wayne asked urgently. "What did he do to her?"

Salty rubbed his swarthy face. "Who knows what goes on behind closed doors, but most of the time the guys don't do anything so terrible. They just keep living too long. The wives get sick of them. They start to feel trapped and unappreciated. You ever hear of black widows?" Salty assumed a confidential tone.

Of course Wayne had heard of black widows, but he also wanted to hear what Salty had to say about them.

"No, I haven't," Wayne lied. "Who are they? And what has it got to do with Megan?"

"We got plenty of these black widows floating around down in Florida," Salty continued. "These are young wives who marry old guys for their money. Most of them are just waiting for the guys to croak. Plenty of them have boyfriends on the side, too. Some of the old guys know about it, some don't. It doesn't matter. The guys are still proud to have young, pretty ladies on their arms. But lots of these guys call for our escorts. The young pretty wives are just arm candy. They're not there for their husbands, rarely give them what they need."

Wayne listened to Salty's graphic description of a sordid situation and thought of his sister again. Did she feel that way too now? It was awful to think of. Wayne instantly turned his thoughts back to the case at hand.

"You're saying Megan's another black widow?" Wayne repeated.

"No question about it." Salty winked. "And I know for a fact, from what Tyron told the girls, that Megan hasn't gone near him for the longest time."

Wayne took it all in. It was what he'd thought, too, but it was good to have it confirmed.

"That old guy was one of the lucky ones to be able to afford our girls," Salty added.

Wayne stood up quickly. "I get the picture." He wanted to get away.

"It doesn't mean Megan killed him though." Salty stood up with him. "Listen, why don't you talk to Fillippa?"

"Who's Fillippa?" Wayne spun around.

"She one of the girls that Tyron spent a lot of time with. He asked for her the most. Fillippa's beautiful and sultry, the guy had good taste."

"Where can I find her?" asked Wayne, fascinated.

"Just be a little patient, and I'll get her over here pronto." Salty came up close beside Wayne. "These are good girls. They want to help out. Fillippa's particularly upset that Tyron's gone. You can talk to her down in the clubhouse, at the back of the building."

"Thank you," said Wayne, "that would be wonderful."

"No problem, buddy," Salty assured Wayne. "We're all here to help."

While waiting to see Fillippa, Wayne put a quick call in to Olivia to let her know what was going on.

"I'm at the escort service," Wayne said as soon as Olivia picked up the phone. "There's both good news and bad news. The good news is that this wasn't the escort service Megan worked with. She doesn't know the girls here closely. That's good for her. Less likely that she arranged a hit."

Olivia breathed a sigh of relief.

"The bad news is that Tyron had been using the escort service for almost two years."

"That's a long time," Olivia remarked.

"Yeah, it is," Wayne agreed. "It tells us two things. Tyron must have been addicted to the girls and there was clearly trouble in the marriage."

"Obviously," Olivia remarked.

"The owner here, Salty, claims Megan hated Tyron, didn't go near him for the longest time. I'm waiting here now to talk to Fillippa next."

Olivia's voice suddenly rose a notch. "Who's Fillippa? One of the escorts?"

"That's right," said Wayne. "Seems like she was the one Tyron called for before the others."

There was silence on the other end of the phone.

"You there, Olivia?" asked Wayne, ill at ease.

"I'm just thinking about it," said Olivia in a now distant tone. "There are certainly perks to this job, I guess."

Wayne smiled. "You're not upset, are you, that I'm going to see Fillippa?"

"Of course I'm not upset," Olivia answered, in a tight tone.

"Yes, you are. You're upset," Wayne countered, surprised.

"Do what you have to, see who you want!" Olivia responded.

"This is business, Olivia, it's part of the job." Wayne was both startled and pleased by her response. It charmed him.

"I know it's business, of course," Olivia replied. "But it might have been nice if you'd asked me to be there with you when you saw her."

Wayne paused a moment and thought about it. "Yes, you're right, that would have been nicer," he agreed.

"Well, I'm glad you see that much, at least," said Olivia.

"Me, too," said Wayne, touched by Olivia's reaction, though he had no intention of telling her so.

*

In a few minutes Salty texted Wayne to go down to the clubhouse in the back of the building. Fillippa had arrived. With a sense of apprehension, Wayne made his way to the private quarters of the escort service.

When he arrived Wayne opened a large door which led to a dark room filled with leather sofas, a bar, and assorted chairs scattered about. Wayne looked around and suddenly saw a beautiful, sultry young woman with long, sandy hair at the bar.

"Fillippa?" Wayne said as he walked up to her.

"Yes." Fillippa smiled seductively.

"Thanks for seeing me," Wayne responded.

Fillippa closed her large, beautiful eyes. "Sit down here," she said, patting the barstool beside her. "It's good to be here with you."

Wayne fought a feeling of pride that arose as he sat down beside her. It was easy to see how Tyron had become lured in. These girls were real pros.

"Tell me what you can about Tyron and Megan." Wayne immediately focused on why he was here.

"Tell you about Tyron and Megan?" Fillippa looked put out. "I thought you were going to ask about Tyron and me."

"You were close to Tyron, obviously," Wayne commented.

"I was there with him all the time." Fillippa smiled. "Except when he wanted to make me jealous and purposely called for other girls."

Wayne couldn't help but smile at that thought. "I can't see why you would be jealous of anyone," he said.

"Why thank you," said Fillippa, running her hands through her beautiful hair and along her shoulders and neck. "I really wasn't jealous of the other girls, but it was a game Tyron loved to play."

"Not the nicest guy, I guess?" asked Wayne.

"No, he was fine. He enjoyed playing games and that's what I was there for. I played them with him for all I was worth. He paid well, gave me big bonuses," Fillippa went on. "The arrangement suited me just fine."

Wayne was startled by her response. It jarred him back to the reality of Tyron's life. An old, sick man confined to a wheelchair, playing games with an escort he paid handily.

"Do you know anything about Tyron's relationship with Megan?" Wayne continued, wondering if Fillippa had been jealous of that.

"Not much." Fillippa seemed to toss Megan aside as irrelevant. "We're told not to talk to our customers about their wives or girlfriends, unless they bring it up."

"Tyron didn't bring Megan up much, I guess?" asked Wayne.

"Once in a while," said Fillippa, "but he just said I was much better than her in every way. Once he even said he was sorry he hadn't met me instead of Megan years ago. He would have had a better life."

"Was he kidding around?" asked Wayne.

"I don't think so," Fillippa replied. "I think he meant it and I think he was right. I was always happy and satisfied with whatever he gave me. Megan was not. She wanted more and more from him. It was never enough."

The thought of it depressed Wayne instantly.

"It's a strain on a man when a woman isn't satisfied with whatever he gives, isn't it?" Fillippa purred.

"It certainly is," Wayne agreed. "So, did you hope Tyron would leave Megan for you one day?"

"Not at all." Fillippa looked strange. "I'm too smart for that. I don't ever get involved with my customers or the games they play. "You can't do the job if you get involved, can you?"

Wayne felt a wave of sorrow as he listened to Fillippa talk. Her life was about playing games for money, living off men's unfulfilled fantasies.

"Who do you think killed Tyron, Fillippa?" Wayne got to the heart of the matter. "Was he set up by one of the girls?"

At that Fillippa laughed out loud. "Ridiculous," she insisted. "Tyron was killed by somebody close to him, I'm sure. Besides, he knew it would happen. One night he even told me he wouldn't be around forever."

"No one is," Wayne countered. "He was getting old."

"No, he was telling me something else," Fillippa countered. "I asked him why not. He said that there were too many snakes in his garden. He couldn't keep track of them." Fillippa stopped and looked at Wayne. "Tyron was telling me there were too many people close to him that were filled with poison, wasn't he?"

Wayne was impressed. "Sounds like it," he replied. "You're smart."

Fillippa closed her eyes. "Of course I'm smart. I know what I'm doing. I won't be in this line of work forever. I'm saving every penny I make here to build a better life."

Despite himself, Wayne was moved. "Good for you," he said, "start building it as soon as you can."

"I'd make a terrific detective, you know," Fillippa said then, in a soft tone. "You guys need someone to work with you?"

Wayne smiled. "Not at the moment," he replied. "But there are plenty of other private investigation firms around."

"Okay." Fillippa spun around on the barstool. "What's next now then?"

"Anything else you have to tell me about Megan or Tyron?" asked Wayne.

"I've told you all I know." Fillippa seemed suddenly bored. "That's all you really want of me? Only dirt on Tyron?"

"That's all, that's fine." Wayne stood up. "It's everything I need right now."

"Okay, good-bye then," said Fillippa, swinging away on her barstool and reaching for a drink.

Wayne walked out of the clubhouse slowly. Once out on the street, he had a sudden urge to call Olivia and tell her what he'd learned. He also wanted Olivia to know that his interview with Fillippa hadn't lasted very long. And that even though Fillippa was beautiful, she couldn't hold a candle to Olivia at all.

Wayne felt shaken by his reaction. Of course he had no intention of actually saying that to Olivia. Rather, he'd just call to check in and ask if she'd like to have a routine dinner and go over what they found.

CHAPTER SIXTEEN

Olivia was disturbed to hear that Wayne was spending time alone with an escort. And she was startled by her own reaction as well. What difference did it make who he spoke to? Why in the world did it bother her? It made no sense at all for her to get personally involved with Wayne's life. Olivia flashed on the pain she'd gone through with Todd. Wayne wasn't Todd, Olivia told herself, and their relationship was purely professional, anyhow. He could spend time with anyone he liked, and he should!

While Wayne was interviewing the escort, Olivia wanted to speak to Megan's friends. She decided to immediately put a call into Andrea, the friend Bella had suggested.

When Olivia called, Andrea picked up the phone sounding as though she'd been asleep.

"Who's calling? Who?" Andrea mumbled over and over.

"This is Olivia Wells, private investigator," Olivia repeated several times. "I'm helping investigate the death of Megan's husband."

Finally, Olivia got through. "Oh yes, sure," Andrea exclaimed. "So, why are you calling me, exactly?"

"You're a friend of Megan's, aren't you?" asked Olivia.

"I am." Andrea couldn't deny that.

"Do you have time for a cup of coffee?" Olivia asked.

"Do I have to?" Andrea mumbled.

"It's important," Olivia replied briskly. "We're investigating a crime."

"Okay, okay, where are you?" Andrea drawled.

"I'm at a diner down near the pier," Olivia responded.

"Funny you should suggest that location," Andrea murmured. "I live just a few blocks away."

"Great," said Olivia. "I'm going to Townsends Diner."

"I'll be there in a little while," Andrea said begrudgingly.

*

Olivia waited in Townsends Diner, which was big and clean with many booths. In about twenty minutes Andrea ambled in, dressed in jeans and an old T-shirt, her hair piled high on her head. Olivia stood up from the booth she'd been sitting in and waved at her.

Andrea looked at Olivia for a long while before she wound her way over to the booth. Olivia wondered what she was thinking, what her hesitation was.

"Just let's be sure this is all totally confidential," Andrea said as she slipped into the seat. "The last thing I need now is to have my name splashed all over the news."

Olivia understood her concern, but couldn't guarantee anything. "This is a serious situation," she responded. "Megan could be accused of a crime."

"What crime?" Andrea snapped. "I heard that Tyron's death was declared an accident."

"Officially, yes," Olivia agreed. "But we're beginning to see circumstantial evidence against Megan pile up."

Andrea looked flummoxed. "Sorry to hear that," she whispered. "But I can understand it. Megan isn't always the easiest person to be around. She's probably done a million things that seem suspicious."

Olivia was surprised by Andrea's response. "I heard you're good friends," Olivia mentioned.

"We were good friends," Andrea corrected her. "We had a falling out and then recently got back together again. It's actually happened a few times."

"What caused the falling out?" asked Olivia, fascinated.

Andrea looked around for the waiter to bring her coffee, paying no attention to Olivia's comment.

Olivia tried another tack. "How do you know Megan?" she asked.

"Megan and I were both former escorts," Andrea quipped, "if you know what I mean?"

Olivia didn't know exactly what Andrea meant. "What?"

"It means we both pulled ourselves out of a rotten life," Andrea breathed. "It also means we both know how to be tricky. And how to take care of ourselves."

"You don't trust each other?" asked Olivia.

"It's not that," said Andrea. "Megan never really came clean with me about the whole truth about anything in her life. I mean, if you're a friend you're entitled to the whole truth, aren't you?"

"Of course," Olivia agreed.

"Well, Megan always kept me an arm's length away." Andrea sounded petulant. "I definitely wasn't thrilled with her relationship with Tyron either, and I took the liberty of telling her. She didn't take that well. Never answered my questions, just started defending herself."

"What did she say?" Olivia was fascinated.

"She said it was none of my business and that I didn't know the whole picture, so I should shut up. So I said, well then tell me the whole picture. After that she didn't say another word. I didn't like that. She was always hiding something."

"What didn't you like about her relationship with Tyron?" Olivia needed to find out whatever Andrea knew.

"Megan took Tyron completely for granted," Andrea murmured. "And it wasn't right. That old guy gave her the shirt off his back. She owed him some loyalty, at least."

"Megan wasn't loyal to Tyron?" Olivia was hungry for details.

"That's putting it mildly." Andrea leaned closer to Olivia over the table. "In fact, if you ask me, I'm positive that Megan recently had an abortion! And the baby wasn't his either! That's for sure."

"An abortion?" Olivia's jaw dropped. "How do you know that? Are you positive?"

"Megan's other friends think so too, though no one knows for sure. I told you, Megan can be tricky. She dropped a few remarks about it to another friend, Nellie. Nellie and Megan have always been tight. I know she tells everything to Nellie. This time Nellie was really upset, though, and mentioned it to me."

"So, Megan had someone on the side?" Olivia breathed.

"Sure," Andrea said. "I always thought that, though of course she never said so. One day recently, though, she looked awful when we met for lunch. I asked her what was the matter and she mentioned that Tyron was furious with her. He'd actually gone ballistic and Megan hadn't been able to sleep all night. I asked her what he was so mad about and she rubbed her belly. That stopped me cold. It made me wonder if Tyron found out about Megan's abortion and flipped his lid."

Olivia was stunned by the information.

"Did you ask her if she'd had an abortion?" asked Olivia. "If that was why she was rubbing her belly?"

"No, I didn't! Of course not," Andrea fumed. "If she hadn't mentioned it to me on her own, she was just going to deny it!"

"Is this just rumor or is it true? I really need to know," Olivia exclaimed. "And if there's some other man in Megan's life, we must know who he is. He could certainly be implicated in Tyron's death."

Andrea froze up. "Go talk to Tyron's daughter, Kayle," she whispered. "Kayle was around Tyron more than the rest of the family. She has to know specifics."

"I will," said Olivia, hurriedly. "And how about Megan's friend Nellie? I want to talk to her, too."

Andrea looked skeptical. "Nellie works in a big club as a hostess," she replied. "She's busy all the time. And she's also very loyal to Megan. I doubt she'd tell you everything she knows. Start with Kayle and see where it takes you."

"Okay," Olivia replied. "I'll go see her right now."

*

Fortunately, Kayle was still back at the home when Olivia got in touch with her. Kayle agreed to the meeting without hesitation and Olivia immediately headed back to Tyron's home.

When Olivia arrived, Tyron's home was filled with family and friends back from the funeral. Megan was nowhere to be seen and Olivia wondered where she had run off to. Olivia located Kayle quickly in a vestibule talking to an older woman and interrupted the conversation abruptly.

"So sorry for getting in the way, but I really need to speak to Kayle for a few moments." Olivia felt shaken by what she'd heard.

"No problem at all," said the older woman. "I'm staying here until later this evening. Kayle and I can talk anytime."

After the older woman backed away, Olivia suggested that she and Kayle go somewhere private to talk.

"There's no place private here right now," said Kayle. "We can go down to the beach for a few minutes, if you like?"

"Yes, fine," Olivia agreed, as they both turned out of the house and back down to the ocean that had grown rougher as the day went by.

"What's wrong?" Kayle asked as they got close to the water and she plopped herself down on the sand.

Olivia sat down beside her. "I'm hearing all kinds of things about Megan," Olivia started, "and I need corroboration about what I hear."

Kayle perked up immediately at that. "Great!" she exclaimed. "I'm glad the truth is coming out finally and she's going to get what she deserves!"

"What truth, Kayle?" asked Olivia. "It has to be substantiated or it won't hold up in court."

Kayle paused for a moment. "You're telling me I'll get into trouble if I can't back up whatever I tell you, right?"

"That's definitely true," said Olivia. "False accusations make matters worse. They waste time, lead investigators astray."

"Okay, so ask me what you want. I'll tell you what I know." Kayle seemed a bit more subdued.

"I've heard a rumor that Megan might have been pregnant and had an abortion recently," Olivia began.

Kayle smiled. "I wouldn't be at all surprised," she whispered.

"Had you heard that yourself?" Olivia wanted to know.

"Something." Kayle shrugged, afraid to speak her mind now.

"You don't know for sure, though, that Megan had an abortion?" Olivia went on. "Your father didn't say anything to you about it?"

"No, my father didn't say that exactly," said Kayle, "he just seemed more and more upset around Megan recently. It figures she might have had an abortion, though. She wasn't around much these past few months. We all wondered why. Where was she? When I asked my father where she was, he only said he was very glad she was gone."

"I'm sorry to hear that," Olivia replied.

"It's not worth being sorry for my father," Kayle quickly replied. "He wasn't exactly an angel. While Megan was gone these past months, he had even more girls than ever coming in and out, taking good care him."

Olivia shivered. "The visits from these escorts had gone on for a long time, right?"

"Yes, they had." Kayle confirmed that it was common knowledge.

"And that didn't bother you?" Olivia began to feel edgy.

"Of course it bothered me," Kyle suddenly blasted out. "But what could I do about it? And who knows how much money he gave these girls? That's money that should have belonged to me!"

"Wasn't your father generous with you as well?" Olivia asked.

"No, he definitely wasn't!" Kayle's grating voice rose in the wind. "I came last, after everyone! His own flesh and blood. I should have come first with my sister, Lana. And my mother should have been important to him, too."

"That's rough," Olivia agreed, suddenly wondering whether Kayle might have been the one who finally decided to do something about this. Was she the one who took matters into her own hands and pushed her father down the stairs?

"How did you handle your upset about all these extra girls visiting your father, Kayle?" Olivia asked.

"I didn't handle it." Kayle grew restless. "I just lived with it! What else could I do? My mother just lived with it too! She hated it! My mother kept saying that my father was making a fool of himself and of us all."

"Were your father's escorts the reason why Megan had someone else on the side?" Olivia persisted.

"Frankly, I don't know or care!" Kayle ran her trembling hands over her face. "I don't care about anything Megan did. She was a dark cloud that fell over our lives and broke up our entire family. She took my father away from me."

"How can I find out if Megan had an abortion?" Olivia whispered.

"Go ask Megan's best friend, Nellie," Kayle quickly replied. "Nellie knows every little thing about Megan. She'll definitely know if this story is true."

"I'll go see her right away," said Olivia.

"If she'll see you, that is." Kayle smirked.

"Nellie has to see me," Olivia exclaimed, "whether she likes it or not. Or else she's obstructing justice."

"I'm not sure that's going to mean a damn to her," said Kayle, "but you go and find out."

CHAPTER SEVENTEEN

The club Nellie worked at didn't open until early evening. After Olivia's call, Nellie agreed to meet her there half an hour before work started. Olivia was meeting Wayne for dinner that evening and she called and asked him to come to the club. He could arrive after Olivia spoke with Nellie and then she and Wayne could have dinner there. It would be the perfect way to go over all that had transpired.

The club Nellie worked in was upscale and flashy with a long red runner that led up to the front door. The entrance was flanked by pine trees with a large billboard over it, announcing who would be performing that week. Nellie had said she'd be inside waiting, but she couldn't stay with her long. Olivia made a point of arriving early, to get as much time as possible.

When Olivia arrived Nellie was sitting at the end of the bar, looking annoyed. She was beautifully dressed and coiffed, as a hostess had to be. Naturally, Olivia recognized her immediately.

"Thanks for getting here early." Olivia walked straight up to her immediately.

"I hope Megan knows that you're here speaking to me." Nellie was aloof. "I tried to call her and tell her, but she didn't pick up."

"Actually, Megan doesn't know that I'm here with you." Olivia was taken aback by Nellie's abrasive style.

"You're working for her, though, aren't you?" Nellie's eyes flashed. "Why wouldn't she know? I'm not doing anything behind her back!"

"I am working for Megan," Olivia replied starkly, "and my task is to find out who killed Tyron."

Nellie looked Olivia over carefully. Olivia was fully prepared for her, too. She'd dressed for the occasion, wearing a fashionable, well-fitting, lime silk dress. With her long hair brushed over her shoulders, Olivia knew that she looked pretty and chic. She was certainly not the image of a private investigator Nellie might have expected.

"Where did Megan find you?" Nellie looked skeptical. "How long have you been in the business?"

"Long enough," Olivia quipped.

"Well, I hadn't heard anyone say that Tyron's death was determined to be a murder." Nellie tacitly refused to go along.

"Evidence is building in that direction, though." Olivia knew she had to shake Nellie up, get beneath her carefully constructed veneer.

"What evidence?" Nellie was startled by the idea.

"I'm not at liberty to say, of course," replied Olivia.

"So you've got all the cards stacked on your side, and I have none?" Nellie looked disconcerted. "That doesn't work for me. I'm supposed to tell you everything and you stay tight-lipped?"

"It doesn't matter what works for you or not." Olivia became steely as well. "This is bigger than both of us. And I need your help."

Nellie got up reluctantly then and shook her head in wonderment. "It is bigger than both of us," she agreed. "Okay, let's go to the cocktail lounge on the side and talk."

Olivia followed her into a large, dimly lit room which was empty now. There were small velvet seats and sofas strewn around for the many guests who were sure to be arriving in a little while.

Nellie immediately sat down on a small sofa and crossed her long legs.

"Ask me what you want and make it fast," she ordered. "My shift is starting soon."

There was no reason to beat around the bush. "What can you tell me about Megan's abortion?" Olivia boldly exclaimed.

"What the hell are you talking about?" Nellie lips pursed tightly and she looked displeased.

"I heard that Megan had an abortion recently," Olivia repeated coldly, as if it were a well-documented fact.

"Well, if she did I know nothing about it." Nellie looked away.

From her taut, angry manner, it was easy for Olivia to see that Nellie knew a great deal. She was hiding whatever she knew, though. Hiding it in plain sight.

"What else can you tell me about Megan's life, Nellie?" Olivia pressed onward.

"What do you want to know?" Nellie now suddenly acted nonchalant and bored. She was like a chameleon, Olivia thought, changing to suit her needs at the moment. Olivia had to pierce through.

"You must tell me who Megan was seeing on the side." Olivia tried another tack.

"Megan never said a word to me about seeing anyone," Nellie said. "If she was, I know nothing about it."

"You're lying to me, Nellie." Olivia suddenly flared up. "It's common knowledge that Megan was unhappy. And you're her best friend. I heard that she told you everything."

Nellie's nostrils flared. "Who told you that? Tell me immediately!"

"Withholding evidence is a criminal offense," Olivia warned.

"This isn't a criminal investigation, though," Nellie persisted.

"But it's about to become one shortly." Olivia remained staunch. "And if you don't cooperate, then you will be complicit. It won't go well for you. I hope you realize that."

"Okay, okay." Nellie suddenly became nervous. "What do you want from me? What do you want from Megan? Tyron was awful to her for two years. He drove her crazy day by day!"

"How?" Now they were getting somewhere. Olivia was excited.

"Tyron flaunted those stupid girls in front of Megan's face. He made a public display of himself and made her look ridiculous, like a fool of some kind."

Olivia breathed loudly. She couldn't deny that was awful.

"And on top of it"—Nellie's voice rose—"Tyron threatened Megan every day that he was going to disinherit her. How much can one person take?"

"Why did he hate her so much?" asked Olivia. "What did she do?"

"It wasn't Megan," Nellie protested. "It was Tyron's life, his sickness, all the stupid choices he made."

"What stupid choices? His marriage to Megan?"

"Maybe." Nellie shook her head hard. "And the lousy business dealings he was involved with, the shady folks he hung around with. Everyone on the take. And don't forget the fact that he'd left his daughters in the lurch all these years. Things like that come back to haunt you."

"Yes, they do," Olivia agreed. "And was Tyron also upset that Megan was seeing someone else? Someone younger, maybe? Did he sense it somehow? Was she making a fool of him, as well?"

Nellie had had enough. She jumped up and got into Olivia's face quickly. "Listen, I wouldn't blame Megan for doing anything she did. She had a right to have a boyfriend, with Tyron and his lousy family treating her the way they did. Including his stupid ex-wife, Alice, who wouldn't leave Tyron alone. Given the hell Megan was living in, I wouldn't blame her for finding someone to love. Why do you blame her? Wouldn't you do the same thing?"

Olivia felt startled and wondered if she would.

"Any woman would, it's not such a big deal." Nellie's face was flushed red. "And I also wouldn't blame Megan for getting rid of Tyron either, if it came to that! I'm not saying she did kill him. I'm saying I wouldn't blame her if she did. Why shouldn't she?"

"She should kill him before he disinherited her, right?" Olivia exclaimed.

"Crazier things have happened," Nellie murmured. "Look, there was not even one person in that family who gave a damn about Megan. Except Alice's husband, Clay. Clay saw what was going on and felt badly. When Alice kept coming to visit Tyron, Clay started to get annoyed. Finally, he started to accompany her. Soon Clay and Megan got to know each other and became friends. Go ask Clay if you want more information."

"That's a good idea," said Olivia. "I definitely will."

Nellie jumped up off her seat then and smoothed out her dress. "Okay, I've got to go to work now. I can't say it was nice meeting you, though! I can say, smarten up!" And she dashed off.

Olivia felt shell-shocked after Nellie left. She was a ruthless character, despite her fancy front. Had Nellie advised Megan to kill Tyron? What was her own life like? Did Nellie carry around a deep desire for revenge?

As Olivia sat there musing, to her surprise Wayne walked into the cocktail lounge. He looked wonderful, dressed in a linen summer jacket and open shirt, and happy to see her.

"How did you find me here?" Olivia jumped up. She thought they were meeting in the front of the club.

"I got here a little early." Wayne smiled. "I just walked into the place and asked where you were. The hostess happened to know you and said you were waiting here in the cocktail lounge."

"The hostess is Nellie, Megan's best friend. She's the woman I came here to interview," breathed Olivia.

"She seems lovely," Wayne remarked.

"Just the opposite," Olivia declared. "She's a tough, tight-lipped customer. I could hardly get anything from her except that I should go speak to Alice's husband, Clay."

Wayne looked surprised. "Clay?"

"Yes, Nellie said that he and Megan were friends, and he was the only one in the family who cared about her at all."

"It's not a bad suggestion then," Wayne concurred.

Olivia looked at Wayne gratefully. Being with him calmed her down instantly. His steady, careful, caring manner was a welcome break from the chaos that was spinning around. Olivia was especially glad Wayne was here now as there was so much to discuss.

"Seems like we have a lot to fill each other in on," Wayne started. "Let's go get a table and have dinner and talk."

They left the cocktail lounge immediately and oddly enough had to wait up front for a few minutes for Nellie to seat them at a table for dinner.

"Just follow me," Nellie said when it was time to be seated. She spoke entirely to Wayne, not even giving Olivia a glance. "There happens to be a lovely table for two in a spot I'm sure you'll enjoy."

"Thanks so much." Wayne smiled appreciatively as they followed Nellie to the side of the club and were seated at a lovely table beside a small, indoor waterfall.

"The waiter will be with you two in a moment," Nellie said before pausing to look at them with curiosity.

"This is my partner, Wayne," Olivia explained. "Wells and Darrington Investigations."

"Oh, I see," said Nellie as she quickly backed off.

The waiter soon arrived and took their orders, and Olivia and Wayne were finally left alone.

"You go first," Olivia said, taking a sip of the glass of ice water on the table. "What did you learn from the escort you were lucky enough to have time alone with?"

Wayne grinned. "You actually sound miffed by it," he mentioned, not letting Olivia's comment pass by.

Olivia smiled as well. "No, I'm just teasing. I mean, it's natural. All guys love spending time with these escorts, don't they?"

"Not all of us," Wayne replied quickly. "As for me, I'd much rather be here, spending time with you."

Wayne's comment took Olivia aback. He seemed to truly mean it and she didn't know what to say. It wasn't what she'd expected to hear.

"Thanks for that," said Olivia, brushing the comment off.

"I mean it, Olivia." Wayne was intent upon making his point, startling her once again.

"Why?" Olivia couldn't help ask. "What's so good about spending time with me?"

Wayne grew silent. "I hope you don't really mean that?" he murmured.

Olivia grew uneasy. Obviously what happened with Todd had taken a bigger toll on her than she'd realized. It had become hard now to trust.

"I don't really feel that way about myself," Olivia spoke up lightly. "I'm just flummoxed with all that's been going on." Actually, Olivia felt deeply touched and reassured by Wayne's comment. She hadn't expected to care this much about it either.

"I would never have asked to be your partner if I didn't think you were special in every way," Wayne went on firmly. "It's an honor to work with you, Olivia, and to be with you now, at your side."

Olivia suddenly felt sad. "Thank you," she whispered, as the waiter quickly appeared with glasses of wine for them before dinner.

A moment of silence fell between Olivia and Wayne as they picked up their wine glasses. She wanted to quickly break into the intimacy that was starting to form. It was too unexpected.

"Okay, really now, let me know what you found out from the escort service." Olivia returned to professional mode. "Then I have tons to tell you as well."

"Unfortunately, I didn't come up with much." Wayne complied instantly. "The head of the escort service, Salty, let me know that Tyron had been seeing these girls for a long while. Everyone knew about it, too. Seems like it was no big deal. And thankfully, the service was not the one that Megan had worked for, so that was good."

"At least one thing lines up on her side," Olivia muttered.

"The escort I interviewed, Fillippa, was one of Tyron's favorites," Wayne went on. "Naturally, she can't stand Megan. She said she was upset by how Megan treated Tyron and the fact that Megan was away a lot."

"What business was it of hers?" Olivia was annoyed.

"Lots of escorts can't stand their customers' wives, I imagine," Wayne replied. "I'm sure they get an earful about them. And they must also get attached to these guys, in their way. Of course, Fillippa claimed that it was purely business for her, that's all."

Olivia shuddered. "Impossible," she agreed.

"You've got to feel bad for them too, though," Wayne added then. "What drives them to this kind of life? Fillippa said she was hoping to save up money and leave the business one day."

Olivia nodded. "I hope she does."

"How about you?" Wayne drank all of the wine in his glass quickly. "What have you got for me?"

"I found out a lot," Olivia started slowly. "I'm not sure it's all true, but we've got to look into it fast. I spoke to two of Megan's friends and checked in with Tyron's daughter Kayle, too."

"Good work." Wayne looked impressed.

"One of Megan's friends, Andrea, thinks Megan recently had an abortion," Olivia finally declared.

"An abortion?" Wayne looked startled.

"Yes, and she thinks Megan was involved with someone on the side."

Wayne tapped his hands on the table. "Unfortunately, it all adds up. It makes sense, doesn't it?"

"Yes, it does," Olivia was sad to say. "And Megan's other friend, the hostess you just met, Nellie, wouldn't give me the time of day. Said she didn't know if Megan had a boyfriend and knew nothing about an abortion either. I didn't believe anything about her. She was defending Megan from the get-to. Nellie did say that Tyron treated Megan horribly, though, and she wouldn't blame Megan for anything at all. Including killing him."

"Whew! Quite a comment. How did Tyron treat Megan horribly?" Wayne was transfixed.

"Nellie said that not only did Tyron flaunt his girls around, he also threatened to disinherit Megan."

"Wait a minute, now. Hold it there. That's a huge claim." Wayne's jaw clenched. "All of these claims are. If any of them are true, it could be that Megan's days as a free woman are numbered."

Olivia couldn't help but agree. "Who isn't against Megan?" she asked.

"No one, except for Alice's husband, Clay," Wayne commented. "Didn't Nellie say that he was the only one in the family who cared at all about her?"

"That's right," said Olivia.

"I think we need to hear more of the other side of the picture," Wayne went on. "Let's get in touch with Clay right away and go talk to him."

Olivia loved the suggestion. "Let's do it."

"In fact, I'll call him right now," said Wayne as the waiter approached with large platters of baked salmon, sliced potatoes, and salad.

As the waiter placed the delicious plates on the table, Wayne quickly got Clay's number and dialed it immediately.

"Clay lives in Key Largo," Wayne announced, as he waited for him to pick up the phone.

Olivia slowly took a bite of dinner, as Wayne spoke into the phone.

"Hi, Clay, thanks for picking up," Wayne said after a few minutes. "This is Wayne Darrington, private investigator." Then he paused a moment. "My partner, Olivia, and I really need to see you badly," Wayne continued, a sense of urgency growing in his tone.

Olivia wondered how Clay was responding on the other side. Would he end up being just another one in the lineup against Megan?

"Sounds great," Wayne suddenly said, excitedly. "We'll leave first thing in the morning, and should get there about ten o'clock."

CHAPTER EIGHTEEN

First thing the next morning Olivia and Wayne were on their way to Key Largo. They decided to take the short flight down there, rather than drive. All in all the flight would only take about an hour.

It was good to get out of Naples for a while and also have uninterrupted time alone with Wayne. As the plane took off, Olivia couldn't help but think of her flight down to Florida with Todd. It was hard to realize that things had changed so drastically in a relatively short while. Todd was gone and Olivia was actually coming to terms with his horrible death. It was Wayne at her side now. In so many ways Todd and Wayne were very different. In others, the same. Both Todd and Wayne loved adventure and were always uplifting and inspiring. Unlike Todd, thankfully, it didn't seem as though Wayne was drawn to shady women. Wayne was tremendously independent as well. Olivia had been wondering if he missed working on the police force. It hadn't seemed so.

Wayne now sat beside Olivia riffling through an in-flight magazine.

"You really enjoy working independently as a detective, don't you?" Olivia asked Wayne lightly.

"Yes, it's great to have the freedom to come and go," Wayne replied. "I like making my own decisions, too, not having to answer to a boss."

Olivia enjoyed that aspect of the work as well.

Wayne put the magazine down on his lap, turned to her, and smiled. "And, as I said before, I really enjoy working with you, too." He was being playful now.

Olivia smiled. "I enjoy it, too," she replied, feeling much easier about it all now.

"Great," Wayne remarked. "It bothered me last night when you asked what was so good about being with you. That's a crazy question."

Olivia took his comment in stride. "I guess it was," she agreed. "I was overtired last night, had too much to process on the case."

"Of course, I get it," Wayne answered, putting his hand on hers briefly and then quickly pulling it away. "I've been there too. It's part of the job, times of total overload. But they inevitably pass and things become clear."

Olivia turned and looked out the window at the light, billowy clouds they were flying through. Right now, the overload was behind her, and she felt good flying through the sky with Wayne.

*

As soon as Olivia and Wayne landed they took a cab straight to Clay and Alice's residence, which was located right on the water, not far from the airport at all.

The home was located down below a small hill which was bordered by a wooden fence, tall bushes, and wild dune grass. It was natural, beautiful, and isolated down here. The cab had to let them out at the top of the hill, and they walked carefully down the hill to get to the front door.

As they walked, the sound of waves, coupled with the strong ocean breezes, washed over Olivia, invigorating her deeply. "What a wonderful place to live," she murmured.

"Clay's a lucky guy," Wayne commented.

"How do you know?" Olivia was surprised by his comment.

"If you wake up every morning in a place like this, you're definitely lucky," Wayne added.

They got to the bottom of the hill and walked a few steps further to the front door. It had been left open for them, but Wayne reached over and rang the bell anyway.

"The door's open, come in!" Clay called from inside. "I'm coming. I'll be right there."

Olivia and Wayne stepped in gingerly. The place was as beautiful inside as it was outdoors. Huge glass windows overlooked the ocean and the wooden plank floors were uncovered by rugs. A few handmade wooden pieces of furniture stood here and there.

"Good to see you." Clay came loping into the room, wearing jeans, a T-shirt, and a huge smile. He could have been a poster child for a surfer, thought Olivia, all toned and suntanned.

"Good to see you, too." Wayne extended his hand to him. "You've got a fantastic place here! Gorgeous."

Clay liked that. "Thanks so much. I love it. My studio is here too, right down the hall."

"What kind of studio?" asked Wayne, swept up in Clay's excitement.

"I'm a sculptor," said Clay as he pointed around. "And all of this is thanks to Alice, too. She set me up in my studio and helped me get the word out about my work."

"Alice is funding you?" Olivia joined in.

"Yes, she is." Clay smiled at Olivia exuberantly. "But she's made a great investment and getting wonderful returns. "My work is really selling now. Soon I'll be able to pay back every penny back she's laid out." Clay looked proud of his accomplishment.

"Fortunate," Wayne remarked, looking around "Is Alice here too, now?"

Clay ran his hands through his long hair. "Not right now," he said. "She's actually been away for a day or so. It seems that after Tyron's funeral, she desperately needed time alone. I expect her back this evening, or early tomorrow at the latest."

"I can understand her needing time alone," Olivia chimed in.

"Yeah, me too." Clay smiled at Olivia again. "I can understand everything. I give Alice all the space she needs and she does the same for me."

"Terrific arrangement," Wayne commented. "Pretty rare too, I'd say."

"I guess it is." Clay suddenly sat down on a long, wooden bench that was standing in front of them and stretched his legs out on a nearby footstool. "Come on, sit down," he said, inviting Olivia and Wayne to make themselves comfortable as well.

"So, it sounds like you've got a fantastic marriage," Wayne continued as he and Olivia pulled over chairs to join Clay.

"Sounds like to who? I wouldn't say exactly fantastic." Clay smiled oddly then. "I'd say my marriage is good, very good indeed!"

"Why not fantastic?" Olivia laughed.

"Fantastic is something else! It's up in the clouds! Heavenly! Breathtaking!" Clay laughed. "Is that even possible in a marriage?"

"I'd say no," Olivia agreed. "Very good is excellent."

"I'd say fantastic is possible!" Wayne interrupted. "Actually, it has to be. Why not? I believe it's possible to love someone so much that you can call your marriage fantastic!"

Both Clay and Olivia stared at Wayne. "Ever been married?" Clay asked Wayne.

"No, I haven't," Wayne confessed, "not yet."

Clay laughed louder then. "No wonder you're not married yet if you think that way! Once you're married you see things differently."

“Were you married before, Clay?” Wayne asked.

“Yeah, I was once, actually,” Clay remarked. “The marriage only lasted a year, we were both very young and I made every mistake in the book.”

Olivia found Clay fascinating and life giving to be with.

“Is that why you married someone older the second time around?” Wayne wasn’t dropping the conversation so quickly.

“Maybe.” Clay scratched his face slowly. “That and practical reasons, too. I met Alice at just the right moment in my life. My sculpting was taking off a little and I found out how happy the sculpting made me. I couldn’t live without it, actually.”

“You were married to your art then, basically,” Wayne commented.

Wayne’s remark startled Clay. “You could say that, I guess,” he replied.

“And Alice did a lot for your art,” Wayne continued.

“But Alice is beautiful, too, don’t forget that.” Clay suddenly defended his wife.

“What keeps your marriage from being fantastic then?” Wayne pursued it.

Clay sat up straighter and looked Wayne in the eye. “Alice is completely obsessed with Tyron. I had no idea to what extent when I married her. She just can’t get over him marrying a much younger woman and making her look old. Like he’d thrown her away. She can’t get over it! Even today.”

“That has to be annoying,” said Wayne.

“Annoying is putting it mildly,” Clay grumbled. “She talks about it all the time and visits Tyron regularly. After we got married I finally realized what was going on. And I didn’t like it! Once in a while I even wondered if she’d married me to get back at him.”

“That must have made you feel rotten,” Wayne remarked.

“It did for a little while,” Clay remarked. “But I don’t hang onto things for too long. Pretty soon I decided to take charge of the whole situation.”

“How?” asked Olivia, fascinated.

“Well”—Clay grinned at Olivia then, as if they were compatriots—“to start with I began to go with Alice on her visits to Tyron. I couldn’t imagine that Megan liked these visits from Alice either and I wanted to find out why she didn’t put a stop to them.”

“Why didn’t she?” Wayne was glued to every word.

“Basically, Megan couldn’t,” Wayne replied. “Even though she’s smart and beautiful and has got everything going, she’s powerless with Tyron. Her wishes mean nothing to him. Nothing at all! I was shocked to realize it. Megan would ask Tyron to keep Alice away and he flatly refused."

"Sounds like Tyron got off on torturing both wives and playing them against one another," said Wayne.

"Made him feel powerful, I guess," Clay added, getting up off the bench suddenly and stretching.

"Did Tyron mind that you accompanied Alice to his house?" Olivia stood up as well.

"No, he didn't seem to care at all," said Clay. "Tyron and Alice would huddle together in his room. They'd always say their discussions were private. Megan and I would be left in the room outside together. When they came out, sometimes they said they were talking about their daughters. But it was all a total bunch of crap. Megan knew it, too. Believe me, she's not stupid."

"Maybe Tyron was also attached to Alice?" Olivia wondered.

"Not at all." Clay smirked. "Tyron basically couldn't care less about anyone but himself. When he and Alice came out of the room, he would throw me a nasty look, as if he'd won."

"Maybe he did," Wayne remarked.

Clay scowled. "Wrong. Alice doesn't love Tyron, she's obsessed with her own pride. In fact, she loves having younger guys go after her. She has plenty of them she hangs out with down at the club."

"Guy friends?" asked Wayne.

"Sure," said Clay. "Why not?"

"And that doesn't bother you?" Wayne continued.

Clay laughed. "Why should it? I'm the one she cares about and everyone there knows it."

"So why does she keep running back to Tyron?" Olivia jumped in, fascinated.

"Megan told me that Tyron was pissed at Alice for marrying a younger guy. That made her happy. She loved seeing him caring about her in any way."

"Why did that upset Tyron so much?" Olivia continued. "After all, he did the same."

"Tyron thought I'd married Alice just for her money. Megan even said that Tyron tried to get Alice to leave me in the lurch!" Clay laughed loudly then. "That wasn't going to happen, of course. Not while I'm still breathing."

The fervor with which Clay spoke startled Olivia. It even seemed as if Clay was implicating himself as he spoke.

"Sounds like you were pretty upset with Tyron yourself," Wayne commented, sharing Olivia's concern.

"Not that upset!" Clay threw Wayne a rough glance. "The old jerk didn't warrant that. I just got sick of Alice visiting him all the time. It started to make me queasy."

Olivia now walked slowly around the room, looking for anything she could see that might give her a clue about what really went on.

Suddenly, Clay walked up close beside Olivia and accompanied her on her stroll. "Looking for something in particular?" he asked.

"Not in particular," Olivia answered lightly. "Just wondering where Alice's things are. I don't get a sense of her presence here at all."

"This part of the house is my studio area," Clay responded. "Alice's quarters are on the other side."

"You guys live separately?" Wayne was startled.

"No, not at all," Clay answered. "I work here and we live over there. But if you want to know the truth, I have been staying on my side of the house since Tyron died."

"How come?" Olivia was alerted.

"Alice has really gone over the deep end since Tyron's death. She's become even more paranoid than before."

"Paranoid about what?" Olivia stopped close to Clay, confronting him.

"In fact, there have been times when she's even threatened me," Clay continued. "She asks me over and over about the time I spend with Megan at the house while she and Tyron are visiting. What about it? I ask. Then she gets crazy and yells that she doesn't like that we're alone together! I'd better never do it again."

"My God," breathed Olivia.

"Yeah, she's off the deep end," Clay continued. "The other day she lashed out and said she was convinced that I was happy now that Tyron was gone."

"Was she implying that you pushed Tyron down the stairs?" Wayne dove right in. "Maybe she thought you were after his money, too?"

"Stupid idiot," Clay murmured under his breath, looking as though dark thunder clouds had suddenly descended on him. "Frankly, I couldn't give a damn about his money or hers. Before long I'll have so much money from my art that whatever they have will mean nothing to me!"

"Her power over you will be gone then?" asked Wayne.

"It's gone now," Clay muttered. "I see Alice for who she is."

"What happens then, Clay?" Wayne closed in. "Is this the end of your marriage?"

"That's what she fears," Clay burst out harshly. "And if you want the truth, she's driving me to it. She's threatening me and suspecting me of everything. She can drive everyone else crazy if she wants, but it's not gonna be me. I'm not gonna be the next one to bite the dust."

"You think Alice drove Tyron crazy?" breathed Olivia. "You think that's why this happened to him?"

"Could be. How do I know?" snapped Clay.

Suddenly, there was a loud knock outside, as if a tree had slammed against a wall.

"What's that?" asked Olivia, startled.

Clay rubbed his hands over his face. "Could be her, slamming her car door," he said as they heard the knock again.

Then the front door of the house flew open with a crash, as Alice wildly stormed in.

CHAPTER NINETEEN

Alice flew into the room, her hair messy, face flushed, sparks flying from her eyes. Then she stopped a moment and stared at Olivia and Wayne, startled to see them in her home.

"What the hell are you two doing here?" she yelled, outraged.

"Wayne called and made an appointment to see us." Clay spoke with as much calmness as he could muster.

"Talk to who? You, or me?" Alice flailed about. "Nobody told me anything about this visit."

"I tried to call and tell you, but there was no answer," Clay said flatly. "You couldn't be reached."

"Who cares if you called or not?" Alice refused to be consoled. "It's over anyway, isn't it? Whether they're here or not won't change a thing."

"What's over?" Olivia jumped in quickly, wanting to settle Alice down. "Did you find out what happened to Tyron?"

At that Alice stopped cold. "What do you mean what happened to him? He's dead, that's what happened. Everyone knows it."

"Olivia means did they find out who did it?" Wayne joined in the fray. "Do they know who pushed him down the stairs? Who has the most to benefit from his death?"

Alice's eyes narrowed. "Plenty of people have a lot to gain from Tyron's death. Don't think you're the only ones investigating the case either. Everyone connected to him is searching for clues. In fact, my daughter Lana has hired her own lawyer and I'm doing my own footwork, too."

"What exactly have you been doing?" asked Wayne, trying to quiet her down. "We'd love to know."

"Oh, would you?" snapped Alice.

"Yes, of course," Olivia joined in.

Alice spun directly toward Clay then, opened her bag, and pulled out a bunch of papers.

"The game is up, Clay," she shouted. "It's over. "See these papers! They tell the whole story."

Clay's eyes clouded over as if he'd been through scenes like this with her many times. "What's over?" he asked. "What did you find now? A receipt for a golden bracelet that ties me to a secret lover?"

Alice rushed over and slapped Clay in the face as he grabbed her trembling hand.

"You cut that out or you're in big trouble!" he muttered. "I've had enough."

"You've had enough? How about me? Before you know it, you'll be out on the street, like you were when I met you," she hissed.

Clay's eyes glared. "No, you got it wrong this time! No one's throwing me anywhere. I'm making a good living now, Alice."

"So you don't need me anymore, right?" she snapped.

Olivia wanted to stop the conflagration between them which was growing more and more intense. She was disturbed by the slap as well.

"What did you find, Alice?" Olivia took a step closer, trying to pull Alice away from Clay. "What's in these papers?"

"Papers don't lie, neither do photos," Alice moaned. "Here's evidence, in black and white, that Clay and Megan were sleeping together. They spent the night together in Mexico City. Not only do I have the hotel receipt. I've got a photo."

Clay blanched as Alice thrust the papers in his face, and he looked at the photo.

"How the hell did you get this?" he breathed.

"Your friend Hank was down at the hotel that time too." Alice was irate. "He took the photo of the two of you. Remember?"

"Vaguely," Clay barely spoke. "But I have no idea why he showed it to you. What's he getting out of that?"

"This isn't about Hank," Alice sputtered. "You and Megan have been cheating on me behind my back! I thought so. I knew it all the time!" Alice was so incensed she could barely speak. "This is how you thank me for all I've done for you? More humiliation?"

Clay said, seemingly unconcerned, "Alice has a funny way of finding evidence and throwing it at me. Just because I was down there at the hotel when Megan was doesn't mean we were sleeping together."

"Give me a break," Alice muttered.

"Why in hell would Megan and I go all the way to Mexico City to spend the night?"

"You tell me that!" Alice demanded.

Clay smiled. "This is paranoia," he murmured to Wayne. "The question is why in hell did Hank show Alice these pictures?"

"Hank's my friend now, not yours," Alice spit back at him. "Did you and Megan plot to get rid of Tyron so you two could finally be together?"

"It's a living hell to be with someone who has paranoia," Clay continued.

Alice wouldn't be stopped, though. "If you both got rid of Tyron, you'd have even more money then, wouldn't you? You'd have Megan's inheritance too!" she added.

"Dream on, dream on," Clay muttered.

"Let me see the papers and photo, please?" Wayne asked then.

To Olivia's surprise, without a moment's hesitation, Clay gave them all to him.

"They don't mean a thing," Clay said under his breath. "Just because she and I happened to end up at the same hotel isn't proof of anything. Even if it were true, even if Megan and I had some time together, there's no proof that we harmed Tyron."

"But you harmed me," Alice yelled. "You harmed me terribly. And I'll never forget it."

Olivia's head was swimming. If Alice's story were true, it could certainly explain the rumors about Megan's abortion. Olivia had no idea if Alice had heard about that yet. She was concerned what Alice's reaction would be when she found out. Even though Olivia would have preferred to remain silent, she knew she had to bring it up. Clay's reaction would also tell them something. For all they knew, news about the abortion could be the golden key to unlocking Tyron's murder.

"Is there anything else about Megan you want to tell me?" Olivia challenged Alice.

"Not really, not at the moment." Alice's eyes flashed. "What are you implying?"

Olivia decided to let the chips fall where they may. "I heard a rumor that Megan might have recently had an abortion," she announced.

A horrible sense of doom suddenly pervaded the atmosphere as Alice began trembling with rage.

"An abortion?" Alice stared.

Olivia then looked over at Clay, whose face had contorted. Was this the first time he'd heard about it? Could it have been his baby?

"Megan would never have an abortion," Clay suddenly exclaimed. "That's not who she is. She just wouldn't do it."

"She would, she did!" Alice turned to Clay darkly. "Megan aborted your baby, and you allowed her to do that?"

"More paranoia," Clay insisted.

"You both went down to Mexico City to have the abortion, didn't you?" Alice added.

"Alice dreams up one grotesque scenario after another." Clay turned to Wayne and Olivia. "But none of them hold up. She loves to implicate everyone in her crazy schemes. Why would Megan and I run to Mexico City? There would have been no need for that." Clay was defending himself beautifully.

"You had a child with her, admit it!" Alice looked both victorious and deranged. "You couldn't have one with me, I was too old for you. I was all used up. So you had one with her!"

Clay got up then and walked to the door.

"Wait a minute, where are you going?" Wayne tried to stop him.

"I don't have to stay here and be assaulted like this," Clay responded. "All kinds of accusations are being flung around and there's no solid proof of anything. Everyone's looking for a scapegoat, but it's not going to be me!"

Olivia felt sympathetic to him. Even if Clay had spent a night alone with Megan, there was no proof that he was the father of her child. Or even that she was ever pregnant. In fact, the idea of it seemed to unnerve Clay as much as it did everyone else.

"Clay's right, this has gotten out of control," Olivia spoke heatedly. "All we have right now are suppositions and rumors."

"Wrong," Alice howled. "I have evidence, real evidence, that Clay and Megan spent the night together in Mexico City."

The phone rang bitterly at that moment, stopping them all midstream. Alice ran over and picked it up instantly.

"It's Lana," she breathed, "my daughter." Alice listened for a while and quieted down. "Okay, I'll tell them," she murmured. "It's good news."

"What is it?" asked Olivia avidly.

"Lana has solid information that will change everything immediately." Alice seemed to calm down a bit more. "She's calling from her lawyer's office."

"Tell us what it is," Wayne spoke up.

"Lana's lawyer just found out that Megan was recently cut out of Tyron's will," Alice declared triumphantly.

"That is news." Olivia was shocked to hear that.

"How's that for motive?" Alice's face twisted. "And here's more, the changes in Tyron's will have not yet been finalized. They were made a few days before he died. Megan had to have found out about it and had him killed!"

The entire room fell silent then.

"The bitch got him in the knick of time," Alice exclaimed. "The money's still hers right now."

"Not if she murdered him," Wayne interjected. "The will is definitely going to be contested."

"It will be contested anyway!" Alice declared. "The question is, did Tyron also write me out of his will? He swore to me he wouldn't. He told me that after Megan got her part, whatever was left belonged to me."

"How about your two daughters?" Olivia suggested. "Tyron could have left his money to them."

"No, he didn't do that! I'm positive of it." Alice sneered. "He told me over and over whatever was left was going to be mine."

"Tyron had many companions, though," Wayne interjected. "You never know who else he promised money to, as well."

Alice glared at Wayne strangely. "That's right, he did have many escorts around. And I knew about every last one of them. But at least when the police hear that Megan was cut out of the will, that's solid evidence against her, isn't it? They'll have to take her in!"

"I'm not sure," said Olivia softly.

"Not sure? You've got to be crazy!" Alice became enraged. "They're taking her in! They have to! It's enough for now. Go home. Go back to where you came from. You're needed there."

*

Immediately after Olivia and Wayne left Clay and Alice's home, they put in a call to Megan.

"Come back up here immediately," Megan demanded. "My lawyer is with me and she says it looks bad. We're swimming in turbulent waters."

"We'll be on the next plane back," Olivia promptly replied.

"Why did you go down there anyway?" Megan was disturbed. "Alice isn't my friend, she's always hated me."

"We wanted to speak to Clay as well," said Olivia.

That bothered Megan even more. "Why Clay?" she demanded.

"We just wanted a new point of view," said Olivia. "Clay seems like a straightforward guy. Different from the others."

"Yes, he is," Megan breathed. "Just get back up here fast and we'll talk."

*

The trip back to Naples seemed to take longer than the one to Key Largo. They were caught in bad traffic on their way to the airport and Olivia feared they would miss the plane. She wasn't looking forward to facing Megan either. Both Olivia and Wayne had some serious reservations about her now. And also some important questions.

Olivia and Wayne sat in the airport waiting to board the flight. Wayne was on his phone with Chief of Police Gallant, listening intently to every word he said. Olivia gazed about, watching families come and go, couples holding hands, old friends reuniting at the gate. She suddenly felt lonely. How had it come to this? Her trips were all about business only. There was never anyone there waiting to greet her with joy on the other end.

Wayne hung up the phone and turned to Megan immediately. "More news," he declared.

"What?" Olivia felt a sudden chill.

"Looks like things are coming to a close," Wayne breathed. "I've seen this happen before, all of a sudden evidence starts rolling in. It's pretty hard to stop the floodgates when they open."

"What else came in?" Olivia felt as though the tide was pulling Megan out to sea. "Is it evidence that looks bad for Megan?"

"It's another piece in the puzzle," Wayne exclaimed. "It's not any one piece exactly that does it, but the weight of them all when they start to pile up."

Olivia shivered. "What is it?"

"Well, as you know, the police have been looking more into Bella recently. It must have made her nervous, because I just heard that Bella came into the police station yesterday with something of her own. She found an old surveillance tape in the basement, of Tyron yelling at Megan for all he was worth."

"Bella suddenly found that?" Olivia was aghast. "Convenient."

"Sounds like she was rattled and looked pretty hard," said Wayne. "She obviously gave the video to the police to take suspicion off herself."

"And the police are buying into it?" asked Olivia.

"It's not about buying into it," Wayne retorted. "They've been watching Tyron on the video, furious with Megan, raging at her."

"Are we looking at a case of domestic abuse?" Olivia wondered if the police had a new take on it.

"You mean do the police think Megan killed Tyron in self-defense?" asked Wayne.

“I wasn’t thinking Megan killed anyone,” Olivia objected when suddenly the loudspeaker announced that their plane was now boarding.

“We’ll find out soon what the police are thinking,” Wayne replied as they went to board their flight. “Bella will be at the station all day. The police are keeping her there for questioning. They want us to come in as soon as we return, look at the video and talk to Bella as well.”

“Sure,” said Olivia, nervously. “We’ll go to the station but first I want to talk to Megan alone, at her home. After all, we’re working for her. She deserves that, at least.”

“She certainly does,” agreed Wayne as the line to board started moving and they quickly stepped onto the plane home.

CHAPTER TWENTY

When Olivia and Wayne arrived at Megan's home, the door had been left open for them and they slipped in. As soon as they entered, Olivia felt a heavy, somber mood all over the place. Not only was it empty, but evening had fallen. By now it was dark and no one had turned on a light.

"Megan," Olivia called out, as they walked around.

Wayne went to a lamp and turned it on as they waited for an answer.

"Are you there, Megan?" Olivia called out again.

Instead of Megan, her lawyer, Cameron Fern, walked into the room defiantly. Beautifully dressed and groomed as before, Cameron had a strange look on her face this time.

"Megan is upstairs in her room," Cameron informed them. "She asked me to tell you both to please go upstairs."

"Thank you," Olivia responded quickly. "Are you coming up with us?"

"No, I'm not." Cameron became jittery. "I've done as much as I can for Megan right now."

"Are you off the case?" Wayne seemed disconcerted.

"I'm not sure." Cameron gave him a long, slow glance and eased up. "There's a lot I didn't know when I took the case on. Now I have to think everything over now. I'm only a divorce lawyer. When things become more complicated I back out."

"Of course," Wayne agreed softly as Cameron smiled at him.

"You're a terrific guy." Cameron's voice became husky as she walked closer to Wayne, getting between him and Olivia. "I thought that about you the second we met."

"Thanks," said Wayne, noncommittally. "Sorry you're leaving the case."

"Well, I may be leaving the case"—Cameron smiled oddly—"but I'm not leaving Naples. You can call any time you like."

Olivia felt a rush of heat flame through her. She couldn't believe Cameron was behaving this way right in front of Olivia's eyes!

Olivia boldly interjected herself. “Why do you want Wayne to call you? Do you want advice about what you should do about Megan? Why not ask Wayne now? Time is of the essence.”

Cameron stared at Olivia, appalled. “When Wayne calls me, I’ll discuss it with him!”

Cameron was obviously trying to push Olivia out of the picture. It wasn’t going to work, though, not now. Olivia threw Wayne a quick glance, curious to see how he would handle this.

Fortunately, Wayne jumped right in. “I think Olivia is making an excellent suggestion,” he agreed. “If there’s anything I can do for you, Cameron, please tell me right here.”

“Really?” Cameron looked offended, gathered herself together, and took off without another word.

As Cameron left Olivia threw Wayne a long glance. “That woman is something else,” she commented.

“I guess I’m just one irresistible guy.” Wayne tried to make light of it.

Olivia knew she should laugh, but couldn’t. Surprised by her own reaction, Olivia realized that she had zero tolerance left for women who tried to get between her and a man she was with. Todd’s cheating had given Olivia a new strength, she realized. She wasn’t about to let it happen again.

“There’s lot of ladies like Cameron around,” Wayne said casually. “Trying to get the guy’s attention and wiping out the other woman is a game they play. It doesn’t mean a thing.”

“It means something to me, though,” Olivia replied briskly.

“I can understand why,” Wayne replied.

Olivia was pleased that Wayne understood and also pleased by his unwillingness to play along with women like that. It was good to see that Wayne wasn’t vulnerable to those kinds of snares.

“Let’s go upstairs and talk to Megan now,” Wayne continued. “She’s alone.”

In the dim light Olivia and Wayne climbed the narrow staircase up to Megan’s room. They hadn’t been up here in her quarters before. Once on the second floor, they walked down a hallway that led to a door that was closed tight.

Olivia knocked on the door. “Megan?” she called.

“Come in,” a muffled voice answered.

Olivia pushed open the door and was startled to see Megan on her knees in the corner of the room, praying. Olivia walked over to her slowly, seeing how distressed she was.

“I’m praying for Tyron,” Megan murmured as Olivia put her hand on her shoulder. “It must have been an awful death for him.”

"I understand," Olivia whispered.

At that Megan turned around and stood up slowly. "Do you really?" she asked. "What do you understand, exactly?"

"I understand that you're in pain," Olivia answered as Wayne came over as well.

"I've been in pain for a long, long time," said Megan in a voice that suddenly sounded like a child.

"We're sorry about that," Wayne chimed in as Megan slowly stood up.

"But sorry's not enough, is it?" said Megan. "It won't help clear my name, will it?"

"No, it won't," Olivia agreed.

"My lawyer's jumping ship too now." Megan turned to Olivia. "Once things go downhill, friends desert you like sinking rats. You can watch them just running away."

"Not all of them," said Olivia, realizing how tough this had to be for Megan. "I'm not going anywhere. Neither is Wayne."

"But the two of you are gathering evidence against me as well, aren't you?" Megan replied.

"I wouldn't put it that way," said Wayne. "We're trying to see things from the largest possible perspective to find out how we can best serve."

"And what if they decide that I'm guilty?" Megan began shivering.

"If things get too bad, there could even be a plea deal available for you," Wayne said softly.

"A plea deal?" Megan was horrified. "Why would I need a plea deal for?"

"The police have now been given a video of Tyron yelling at you," Wayne responded. "It goes to motive. There's just one thing after another."

Megan stumbled over to a nearby lounge and sprawled out on it. "Who gave it to them? Bella, right?"

"Yes, that's right," said Olivia.

"Bella's trying to deflect the attention from herself onto me!" Megan yelped. "Bella's always been possessive of Tyron and incredibly jealous of me and his family. She once even said that Tyron belonged to her, that she was his only real family. Where would Tyron be without her taking care of him? Nowhere!" Megan was now becoming more and more distraught.

"That's not proof that she killed him though," Wayne insisted. "Just the opposite. It sounds like she really cared."

"So, you also think Bella cared about him? You don't think I did, only Bella?" Megan was beside herself.

Olivia wanted to change the focus of the conversation, to calm Megan down and offer another way of framing things. "Did Tyron yell at you often?" Olivia broke in then. "Would you call this a case of domestic abuse?"

At that Megan smiled eerily. "The word abuse doesn't apply in my marriage," she whispered. "Don't even go there. Tyron gave me oodles of money to do with whatever I liked. Anyone who knows that will ask how the marriage was abusive."

"Money can be used in lots of ways," Olivia replied. "Did Tyron control you with his money? Did he think it gave him the right to abuse you?"

"You're smart, Olivia, I'll give you that," said Megan. "But you're wrong there. Sure, Tyron was a bastard and at times I hated him, but I also loved him. We were good to each other in the beginning, before he got sick."

"And afterwards?" asked Olivia.

"After he got sick, Tyron pushed me away a lot." Megan was whimpering. "He was upset and started letting it out on me. He was ashamed of the condition he was in. I can't say I blamed him."

"So you two had an understanding?" Wayne quickly asked. "You would let him see his escorts and he'd let you do what you liked?"

Megan perked up. "Sure. Even before he got sick Tyron never stopped me from doing whatever I liked. He wasn't stupid. He knew there was a huge age difference between us."

"He didn't stop you from seeing other guys?" Olivia asked.

Megan shrugged offhandedly. "We just never discussed things like that, ever."

"Did you see other men during your marriage?" Wayne felt compelled to jump in.

"I did, from time to time," Megan murmured. "It wasn't a big deal. It didn't mean much to me or to them either."

"None of them meant much to you? Nobody?" asked Olivia quickly.

Megan looked over at Olivia carefully. "No," she replied.

"Not even Clay?" Wayne interjected.

At that Megan looked away. "Clay was different," she said softly. "He was the only one who was kind to me."

"That meant a lot, didn't it?" said Olivia, leading Megan on.

"Yes, of course it did. Why wouldn't it?" Megan insisted. "It's not so often you find a guy that's kind."

"That's why you spent time alone with Clay in Mexico City?" Olivia asked.

Megan smiled. "You know about that, too? So what? Is it so terrible? Am I the worst woman in the world? Yes, sure, I spent time with Clay alone in Mexico City. He was kind to me and deserved it."

"Deserved what?" asked Wayne.

"Clay deserved the pleasure of a woman who cared for him." Megan's voice grew ragged. "His life with Alice had become a total nightmare. I saw it myself right under my eyes. He was trapped like I was in a horrible marriage."

"Did you fall in love with Clay?" Olivia had to ask.

"I don't know what falling in love means," Megan answered fitfully. "I told you Clay was kind to me. I was grateful." Megan ran her hands over her taut face. "Neither of us ever said a word about falling in love. Who talks like that anymore?"

"Megan," Wayne obviously decided to up the ante, "did you have an abortion recently?"

A long, sorrowful moment passed before Megan could speak. "I didn't want to," she said, pitifully. "I had no choice about it."

"Why not?" Olivia was electrified. "Who insisted you have it? Did they threaten you?"

"No one threatened me," said Megan, "but there's not always a choice."

"Was it the father of your child who insisted you have the abortion?" Wayne demanded.

"That wasn't the reason." Megan's voice dropped to a whisper now.

"What was the reason?" Olivia had to know.

"It's not your business anyway." Megan flipped her hair off her face swiftly. "I just did it, that's all. And there's no going back now."

"It's an important part of the picture," Olivia continued. "Is that the reason Tyron became so enraged with you? Is it why he was yelling at you like that on the video?"

"Why should Tyron be enraged about it anyway?" Megan's voice became more shrill. "The baby wasn't his. That much is obvious, isn't it?"

"Who was the father? Tell us," Olivia demanded.

"Never." Megan immediately clammed up.

"I believe it was Clay," Wayne interjected.

"Believe what you want! I don't care." Megan turned away.

"It seems like you got rid of the baby because Clay was married to Alice! You're protecting someone! You're protecting him!"

"No," said Megan emphatically. "And it doesn't matter who the father was either. It's irrelevant to everything."

"And maybe it isn't," Olivia exclaimed. "It's possible that the father of your child killed Tyron because he wanted you for his own, isn't it?"

"Nobody wants me for their own," Megan wailed loudly then. "Enough! Enough!" She held up both hands.

"The more you tell us the better it will be," Wayne warned, emphatically. "You're in trouble now, Megan."

"Nothing will ever be good for me, will it?" Megan replied. "I didn't hire you to tell me that I was in trouble. I hired you to find the killer, to clear my name."

"How can we clear your name when one piece of evidence like this comes up after another?" Wayne shot back.

Megan was now trembling. "What other evidence?" she asked in a frightened tone.

"Did you know that Tyron was in the process of cutting you out of his will?" Wayne added.

Megan sighed. "Yes, I knew that," she answered with a strange look of resignation.

"The changes in his will weren't finalized before he died. It was just a matter of days before they would be," Wayne added.

"It's true, it's all true," Megan finally whispered in a harrowing tone. "I deny nothing."

"The circumstantial evidence is overwhelming." Wayne's voice rose. "And the fact that you knew that Tyron cut you out of the will makes things seem incontrovertible."

"Seem is the operative word," Megan muttered, looking pleadingly at Olivia. "The world is not what it seems. It seems like I killed him, but I didn't."

Olivia couldn't help but believe Megan, though she had no sure reason to feel that way.

"The stars are against me." Megan began unraveling. "My destiny is closing in."

"Tell us the full truth, Megan, and we'll do our best," Wayne pleaded.

"What happens next?" was all Megan could reply, crestfallen. "Are the police going to take me in for questioning again?"

"I don't see how they can do otherwise," said Wayne. "Think about a plea deal, please!"

"I don't want a plea deal. I didn't do anything. I'm innocent!" Megan exclaimed.

Olivia and Wayne glanced at each other quickly.

"What about you, Olivia?" Megan turned to Olivia. "You've come through for others at the last minute before! You always find the real killer. Are you going to come through for me as well?"

CHAPTER TWENTY ONE

After Olivia and Wayne returned to their hotel, the call from the police came promptly. Megan was going to be taken in for further questioning first thing in the morning. Bella would be at the station then as well. The police were hoping to wrap up the case fairly soon after that. It was imperative that both Olivia and Wayne be present.

Naturally, Olivia and Wayne agreed. Before they parted for the night, Olivia and Wayne grabbed a quick cup of coffee in the lobby of the hotel.

"Megan looks guilty as hell," Wayne said as he raised his coffee cup to his lips.

"It's too soon to say that," Olivia objected. "I'm still not sure."

Wayne shook his head. "I think you're wrong on this one. Sometimes things go fast and there's no doubt."

"I have doubt, though," Olivia murmured as she sipped her coffee slowly.

"That's your MO, Olivia," Wayne replied. "I'm not saying doubt isn't good, but you can go overboard. Too much doubt can work in the opposite way and blind you to the truth."

"It can," Olivia agreed, "but we have to be positive before we can say that Megan's guilty. And there are plenty of other suspects floating around who haven't been explored."

"Like who?" Wayne seemed annoyed.

"A few," said Olivia. "For starters, what about the people involved in Tyron's shady business dealings?"

"Tyron's business contacts have all been thoroughly investigated by the police and cleared," Wayne replied.

"Okay, so how about his daughters, then?" True to form, Olivia would not let go.

"What about his daughters?" Wayne looked put off. "It's a big stretch to say that they'd kill their father. Nothing between Tyron and the girls had changed recently. And his daughters weren't the ones he was cutting out of his will. Megan was!"

"So, how about the father of Megan's unborn baby? The one she's protecting with her very life." Olivia couldn't stop now even though she knew she was on a fishing expedition.

"That's a long shot," said Wayne. "We don't even know who the father was."

"It seems pretty obvious it was Clay, doesn't it?"

"So, are you suggesting that Clay needs to be investigated?" Wayne was definitely piqued.

"No, not really." Olivia liked Clay and had no sense that he would be involved in a murder. Clay's life was on the upswing now too, and he didn't need Tyron's money. Olivia pulled out the last possibility then. "But I'm not sure why Bella's been let off the hook so easily either," she said.

"Bella's been interviewed numerous times," Wayne said forcefully. "Everyone who knew her said that she meant Tyron only good."

Olivia felt momentarily defeated. She'd been hanging onto the idea that Bella was somehow involved. She hoped that more would come out tomorrow at the station about that. It was at least still a possibility.

"Let's see what happens at the station tomorrow," Wayne said slowly, putting his coffee cup down. "Get ready. I have a feeling that there are surprises waiting and that things will get wrapped up quickly. Right now we both need a good night's sleep."

"We definitely do," Olivia agreed as they walked to the elevator, took it to the same floor, and then, with a brief smile, quickly parted ways.

*

First thing in the morning after breakfast, Olivia and Wayne arrived at the police station. When they walked in both Megan and Bella were already in the interrogation room along with a group of investigators and police.

The moment Olivia entered the room Megan looked up at her tearfully.

"They're all trying to trap me," Megan called to Olivia pleadingly. "They're building a coffin for me that I'll never climb out of."

Bella scoffed at that. "They're not building a coffin," she interrupted, "the truth is speaking for itself."

"What do you know about the truth?" Megan lashed out at Bella fiercely. "You had a job at my home and you did it. You didn't know all that was going on in my life."

"Oh no?" Bella's face suddenly became distorted.

"And I didn't know all that was going on in your life either. Who knows how much money Tyron gave you on the side?" Megan had suddenly found her stride. "Who knows how much you were even stealing from him?"

"Me, stealing?" Bella's eyes opened wide as she turned to Chief of Police Gallant. "She's turning everything against me now to save herself. I never stole a thing in my life."

Furious, Megan wouldn't let go. "Who knows what the escort service slipped you on the side?" she added. "Bella was the one who hired those girls for Tyron. Every single one of them!"

Everyone stopped then and stared at Bella.

"I had to, I had no choice about it." Bella's voice rippled through the stiffening atmosphere. "Megan wasn't there for Tyron! It made him crazy, too. How could she have left her husband alone?"

"Shut up!" Megan lashed out.

"The poor guy needed something, didn't he?" Bella continued.

"He had what he needed," Megan slapped back.

"No, he didn't," Bella insisted. "Why did his wife disappear on him like that? In the beginning it was only once in a while that I needed a girl to fill in for Megan. After that it was more and more. The past few months she wasn't anywhere around! Why not? Did she have someone else she was seeing?"

"She's blaming me to take attention away from herself," Megan shouted. "Bella was the one downstairs with Tyron when he fell to his death."

At that Gallant stepped forward strongly and confronted Megan. "Bella didn't do it, we're positive of that," he announced.

Megan flinched. "Positive?"

"We have more information," Gallant said, a small smile forming around the edges of his mouth.

"What?" Megan asked, shaken.

"We just found the surveillance video of Bella that had been placed in the front of the house. Someone had taken it down and buried it."

"Buried it? Where?" Megan was aghast.

"It doesn't matter where." Gallant's voice grew threatening. "Where we found the video is beside the point. The point is that the video placed Bella in the kitchen, cooking, during the time Tyron was killed!"

Both Olivia and Megan grew silent at the same time. The field of suspects had now greatly narrowed, Olivia realized. Megan was standing alone. All eyes in the room turned to Megan.

"Now, answer me straight," Gallant continued, "and stop putting the blame on Bella. Did Tyron find out you were seeing someone? Is that why he was cutting you out of his will?"

Megan simply stood silently, staring, unable to respond for the moment.

"No, that's not why he tried to cut me out of the will," Megan suddenly burst out. "He did it because he'd hated me for a long time! He was desperate to get rid of me any way he could."

Olivia's thoughts started racing. Tyron had even offered Bella money to have Megan disappear. Olivia wondered if she should mention that now, but didn't know how the police would respond. Would it add to suspicion of Megan? Olivia didn't want to be part of that. This case was a tapestry with many strands woven together. Olivia wanted more time and space to pull the strands apart, one after another.

"Your husband was desperate to get rid of you and you stayed with him anyway?" Gallant's voice dropped as he continued pushing Megan.

"Where was I going to go?" Megan's voice cracked then; she was on the verge of tears.

"There were plenty of places you went to," Bella chimed in, victorious now. "Why didn't you go and stay there forever?"

"Where did you go when you were away so long?" Gallant stepped forward angrily.

"I don't know where I went." Megan began sobbing.

"Of course you know." Gallant looked at her oddly.

"Let her cry all she wants." Bella burst into the conversation. "She knows where she went, just doesn't want to tell you. She went away partying with some guy."

"Is that true?" Gallant turned to Bella then. "Who did she go partying with?"

At that question Bella came up cold. "I don't know who."

"You have no idea?" Gallant pursued it.

"None at all," Bella exclaimed. "But she was gone, wasn't she? Where else would she go?"

"That's an open question." Olivia stepped forward then. "We need time to explore the answers. We need time to find out who Megan was with and what their stake was in seeing Tyron gone!"

"But time is running out fast!" Marcus, another officer there, stepped forward. "Megan obviously knows where she went. There's a reason she's not telling us. Where did you go, Megan?"

Megan looked at him sadly. "I drifted around, went to see this one and that one. There wasn't one place I stayed at. Nobody really wanted me for very long."

Gallant threw Wayne a searching glance. "Did you mention the plea deal I offered to her lawyer?" Gallant asked.

"I did," Wayne replied. "She has no interest in taking it."

"Too bad," muttered Gallant. "We've also been playing around with the original surveillance video of Tyron on the patio. You know, the one that was hard to see, that was tampered with."

"What about it?" Megan spun toward Gallant, now suddenly alarmed.

"We've brought in top experts at reconstruction and are getting much closer to finding out who tampered with it!" Gallant challenged Megan.

"There's no way to find that out." Megan started trembling.

"There definitely is," Gallant answered smugly. "Ever hear about the cutting-edge advances in technology?"

Olivia wasn't sure that was true. Gallant was probably lying to Megan, pressing her, in order to get the whole truth. Whatever he was doing, it was working.

"Okay, okay!" Megan suddenly held her hand up in front of her face. "I can't take it another minute. It's enough, stop it. I did it. I tampered with the video."

"You did it?" Gallant shot back as the entire room froze.

"I did it because I didn't want you to see Tyron screaming at me like he did. He screamed all the time. It was humiliating." Megan was crumbling in front of their eyes.

Gallant shook his head. "It's all over now, Megan," he said.

"But if you look carefully, the video I tampered with was filmed earlier in the day," Megan went on breathlessly. "It was hours before Tyron was pushed down on the sand. Hours! Check it out, please!"

"We still can't see the exact time of day the video was recorded," Gallant replied. "What we do know is that it was definitely filmed the day Tyron died. And that he was screaming at you. And now you say you're the one who tampered with it."

"But I didn't kill him! I didn't, I didn't!" Megan started to shriek.

Chief Gallant nodded to other officers there. "Okay, book her and arrest her. We've got what we've been looking for."

The other officers in the room closed in then, pulling Megan's arms behind her.

"Believe me, someone, believe me!" screamed Megan.

Olivia and Wayne looked at each other, stunned. "She never told us she meddled with the surveillance video," Wayne murmured to Olivia. "She tried to dupe us, too."

"Why would she do that?" Olivia was breathless.

"It was a scam. Megan wanted us to cover for her to take away the heat," Wayne replied. "Cameron was too smart to go for it, though. We should have realized something was wrong when Cameron left the case."

Olivia felt stung. "Well, maybe Cameron's smarter than both of us, but I'm still not entirely sure Megan's guilty."

As the cops dragged Megan away, Olivia saw her turn and throw Olivia a pleading glance over her shoulder.

"I didn't do it," Megan called out again, hoping that just one person would hear her.

*

Olivia and Wayne left the police station soon after.

"So, are we off the case officially now?" Olivia asked as they walked down the long avenue in the balmy summer air.

"In a little while," Wayne answered. "The police will first have to file charges and take care of other details."

"But we're not off the case until Megan says so, are we?" Olivia insisted.

"Not officially, no," said Wayne. "Why?"

"Just wondering," Olivia mused.

"Well, let's do our wondering down near the beach right now," Wayne suggested, running his long fingers through his hair. "It's a beautiful day and we could use some downtime."

"We certainly could," said Olivia, upset by the developments and eager to be near the sky and water with Wayne.

CHAPTER TWENTY TWO

Olivia and Wayne arrived at the beach in what seemed like no time at all. From the police's point of view, the case seemed to be closed and the day could be thought of as an unexpected holiday.

"This is the last place I expected to be this morning," said Olivia as slipped out of her shoes.

"It's great, isn't it?" said Wayne, doing the same. "We both can sure use some downtime at this point."

That couldn't be disputed, thought Olivia as they walked barefooted along the warm sand to the edge of the water. When they got to the shore Olivia watched the waves roll in and slide between her toes. Thankfully, it relaxed her. The tension in the case had been relentless and no matter what the others said, it wasn't over for Olivia yet.

"I love it here," Olivia said, as the breezes washed over.

"I do too!" Wayne agreed.

"I'm still uneasy though," said Olivia, reaching down into the ocean and splashing it on her face.

"I told you this case could finish up quickly," Wayne said as he sat down on the sand and stretched his feet into the waves. Then he turned and with both hands began digging and piling up sand.

Olivia smiled a bit as she watched him. "Are you actually making a sandcastle?" she asked. Wayne had so many sides to him. At times she could see him as a young boy, relaxed and playful. Other times he was completely take charge, focused. A still point in the storm.

Olivia sat down on the sand beside him and began scooping the sand up with her hands as well.

"Looks like we're both building sandcastles," Wayne laughed.

"Guess so," said Olivia. It seemed okay for the moment to take a little break. "But sandcastles get pulled out into the ocean pretty fast," Olivia suddenly added, thinking about the case. They'd all built a sandcastle about Megan's complicity, but how strong was the foundation? Could the case easily crumble and roll away like sand?

"I get what you're saying," said Wayne. "You're referring to Megan."

"I am," Olivia agreed.

"Well, from everything we've seen and heard, it's obvious that she's guilty, isn't it?" he replied, digging more intensely.

Olivia flinched. "I wouldn't say obvious."

Olivia leaned over and quickly pulled up more damp sand. "I'd say it's possible she's guilty, but maybe not?"

Wayne stopped digging abruptly. "Well, that's a big step for you at least, to say that it's possible."

"It is possible, likely even," Olivia added. "But is it obvious? No, not to me. I'm still troubled by Alice and Clay's relationship and how Clay's friend Hank gave Alice that photo. Why would he do that?"

"There's a time when questions like that are over," Wayne spoke forcefully then. "Megan lied to us, Olivia. I can't get past that. Lying is always a sign that's something's terribly wrong."

"She didn't lie to us, exactly." Olivia felt compelled to defend Megan. There was no one else around who seemed to want to.

"Megan withheld important information," Wayne continued vigorously. "That's the same as lying. She never told us that she'd tampered with the original surveillance video."

"You're right." Olivia had to concede that point.

"If Megan was innocent," Wayne continued, "she would have let us know about the video up front and told us why she did it. Instead she purposely kept us in the shadows. That's not good."

"Megan definitely broke trust," Olivia replied softly. "I was surprised to learn that as well."

Wayne stopped and turned completely to Olivia. "Once trust is broken, there's no going back."

Olivia was struck by the intensity of Wayne's feeling. He must have had been through a painful loss of trust himself, she thought. It was interesting how similar they were, Olivia realized. She, too, had no tolerance for breaking trust.

"Was your trust broken a lot in the past?" Olivia asked him as the waves came rippling up onto the sand.

"Of course, many times," Wayne replied matter-of-factly. "It happens to all of us, doesn't it?"

"It does," said Olivia. "But some of us handle it better than others. For some, breaking trust feels like an earthquake. After that, the relationship can never be fixed again."

Wayne nodded. "You're right, you're smart, that's well put. You continually surprise me with your insight."

Olivia was pleased. Despite being on edge, she was thoroughly enjoying their conversation. "I don't handle trust being broken well either," she said. "In fact, I hate it."

"Me, too," Wayne agreed as the waves became more forceful.

"But just because trust was broken between us and Megan," Olivia went on, "it doesn't mean she killed Tyron."

Wayne frowned. "No, but it means she can't be trusted. Other things she told us may also be lies. We don't know what to believe exactly. We can't stand by her word or stand up for it."

"It may be that we don't have the whole story yet," Olivia mused.

"We definitely have enough of the story to draw a conclusion," Wayne insisted, rubbing his heel on the moist sand. "Obviously the police feel that way, too. They have a good enough case against Megan to take her in now."

"But I'm not convinced of it fully," Olivia couldn't help reply.

"Why not?" Wayne was growing irritated.

"Because things are adding up too neatly and too quickly," Olivia remarked.

"Does losing the case make you feel like a failure?" Wayne burst out, not holding anything back.

Olivia was startled by his abrasive remark. "Maybe it does," she had to admit. "What are you getting at?"

"We all feel like failures when our cases collapse," Wayne quickly added. "But you can't give in to those feelings. If you do, you won't last in this line of work. It's never about personal failure or success, it's about finding the real killer."

Olivia realized that she needed to hear that. Once she started taking things personally, she would be lost.

"This is a high-stakes game we're playing." Wayne's voice got louder, as if he were trying to wake her up. "There's only so much that's in our control. We're up against killers and snakes of all kinds. If you've done your best, held nothing back, then no matter what happens, it's a success."

Wayne's sharp comments were right on point. But they also made Olivia feel sad. There were tricks to the trade, she realized, tools you needed, ways of looking at things that made it possible to keep going. Without them, it was easy to get off track.

"Thanks for your insight, Wayne," Olivia said quietly.

"Thanks for listening," he replied. "And it's not some special insight. It's just plain experience speaking. There are points of danger everywhere. One of them is feeling like a failure and letting that force you to keeping going on a case, long after things are done."

"I heard you, I get it." Olivia began to get antsy.

Wayne sighed. "You know, I think we both could use some downtime," he replied. "We've been working so hard, we're wound up in knots. How about planning an evening of dining and dancing? There are some wonderful clubs in Naples."

Olivia smiled. The invitation was tempting. It had been a long time since Olivia had time to just play.

"It sounds like a wonderful idea," Olivia responded. "I'd love to take you up on it after the case is really closed."

"I've got news for you, Olivia," Wayne whispered. "It's really closed now."

"Not for me, not yet," Olivia whispered back, as another large wave rolled in over the sand and on top of the sandcastle Wayne had been building.

"Wow, the waves are getting much stronger," Wayne muttered.

"Yes, they are and we'd better be careful or they're going to pull down everything you've built," Olivia remarked.

"Let them pull down whatever they like." Wayne grinned. "I'll just start again and build something new."

*

After time on the beach and lunch at the hotel, Olivia and Wayne went to their separate quarters for a few hours to have some time alone. After that, they planned to have dinner that evening, in a charming restaurant in Naples. Then Wayne wanted to return to Key West. There wasn't anything left to do here and there certainly had to be other cases waiting for them. He wanted to be where they were needed and could make a real difference.

It was too soon for Olivia, though. She felt jarred by the thought of leaving. "I can't go yet, Wayne," she responded immediately to his suggestion.

"Are you driven to succeed in every single thing you do?" Wayne asked, putting the question slightly differently this time.

Olivia was put off. "Maybe that's part of it," she said to Wayne. "It's only part, though."

"You didn't fail Megan, she failed us." Wayne was suddenly adamant. " Megan failed herself. That's not our fault."

"I'm still not ready to return to Key West yet," Olivia balked.

"Well, we can't stay here forever." Wayne's face grew tight. "Let's take some time alone this afternoon and you think about what you need to be ready to go."

That suited Olivia. "Good," she said. "I'll think it over carefully."

"Please do," said Wayne, "and then, at dinner tonight, you can let me know."

*

Back in her room alone again now, Olivia stepped out onto the patio and wracked her brain to understand why she couldn't go. What was really bothering her? She looked at the floating clouds in the sky above. Each cloud has its own destination, she thought. They all weren't all headed in the same direction. She and Wayne didn't have to agree on everything. She could follow her intuition and he could follow his.

Olivia thought again about Wayne's comment. Was she intent on continuing the investigation because of personal failure? She didn't really think so. Olivia couldn't help but also think of Tyron's fate. His murder had to be accounted for properly. What if Megan wasn't the one who'd harmed him? What if someone else out there was responsible? Should they be let off scot-free? Should an innocent woman get locked up because circumstantial evidence piled up and the conclusion was convenient? If that happened, would Tyron ever be able to rest in peace?

Olivia went over all that had transpired, again and again. What bothered her most, she realized, was that she didn't know who the father of Megan's unborn child was. Why wouldn't Megan tell them? She was definitely protecting him from something. Whoever the father was had to be more complicit than anyone knew.

Once again Olivia's thoughts returned to Alice and Clay. It seemed likely that Clay was the father of Megan's baby. Had Alice found out about that earlier on? Both of them had seemed troubled by the idea of an abortion when Olivia and Wayne had mentioned it. But who knows? They could have been hiding the truth like everyone else. Olivia wanted one more chance to talk to both of them and have her questions answered once again. The second time around was often different.

Olivia realized that she needed to return to Alice and Clay's home in Key Largo for another visit. After that, she'd be able to return to Key West and move on. Relieved that she had an answer to Wayne's question, Olivia went back to her room to dress for dinner. She'd tell him that the visit with Alice and Clay would help her tie things up.

Olivia put on a long, willowy, black, silk summer dress, and brushed her hair over and over. Then she put on a hand-carved necklace and sandals. When Olivia met Wayne down in the lobby, she smiled to see the look of delight on his face as she approached.

"You look fantastic," said Wayne.

"Thanks," said Olivia, "and I have the answer to your question about returning to Key West, as well."

"Really? Tell me when we get there." Wayne looked happy as they left the lobby to get into a cab to take them to the French restaurant in town, which was placed in the middle of a wild garden.

Fortunately, at dinner, Wayne did not bring up returning to Key West immediately. Instead, they enjoyed their meal as he went over details about the case closing.

"We definitely do not have to stay here in Naples any longer," Wayne finally remarked. "There's nothing further left to do."

"Just one more thing," Olivia contradicted him playfully.

"What?" Wayne looked perplexed.

"I want to go back to visit Alice and Clay one more time," Olivia remarked.

Wayne shook his head in confusion. "Why?"

"I just have to," Olivia said. "I'm not satisfied. It seems certain that Clay was the father of Megan's unborn baby. So, why wouldn't she have let us know that? In fact, she was adamant about not revealing who the father was. There has to be something else she's hiding about this as well."

"Megan wasn't forthcoming about anything, really," Wayne responded. "The truth about her entire life dribbled out slowly."

Olivia knew that was true, but it didn't matter. "I still need to talk to both Clay and Alice again," she insisted. I want to find out if Alice knew all along that Clay was the father of Megan's baby."

"And if she did? So what?" Wayne wasn't going along with it.

"Was Clay afraid of what Alice was going to do about it? Was that why Megan was keeping it hidden?" Olivia was glad for the chance to let Wayne know what she'd been thinking. "Megan said she had no choice except to have the abortion. Was pressure from Alice the reason? Had Alice been threatening Megan secretly? Or perhaps it was Clay?"

"This is fantasy and pure speculation," Wayne replied. "If Alice found out that Clay was the father, it's possible that she'd be furious and leave him. What has that got to do with Tyron's death? This is all nothing more than a side show."

"No, you're wrong." Olivia was feeling more and more certain. "Clay was definitely afraid of something too, or Megan would have told us that he was the father."

"It's ridiculous, Olivia," Wayne interrupted. "Clay doesn't need Alice anymore, he has enough money now to live well without her. What kind of danger could there be in this for him?"

"Then why didn't he admit to us that he was the father?" Olivia couldn't let it go.

"Olivia, Olivia," Wayne burst out. "There's a fine line between being a good detective and becoming suspicious of everything."

"I know that," Olivia retorted.

"And what if Clay wasn't the father?" Wayne was upset. "Megan admitted to playing around with lots of different guys, didn't she? And from the way she described her affairs, none of the guys meant much to her either. Didn't she tell us that she was never in love with any one of them?"

"She said that but I don't believe her," Olivia exclaimed. "And I still want to go back there and talk to Alice and Clay."

Wayne became silent. "I can't go along with this. It doesn't make sense."

"That's fine, Wayne." Olivia was steadfast. "You don't have to agree. I'll go myself and talk to them. Then I'll feel satisfied. I'll be able to return to Key West after that. If you want you can go back to Key West while I'm down at Key Largo."

"Okay, I will," Wayne said slowly. "That makes the most sense, doesn't it?"

"It does, it's fine," Olivia assured him. "We don't have to agree about everything. We can each follow the road that calls to us. In fact, we have to."

"You're right," Wayne agreed.

"Okay, then, we have a deal." Olivia was relieved. "I'll go back to see Alice and Clay and you return to Key West. We'll stay in touch and when things are settled, I'll return as well."

"Okay, we have a deal," said Wayne, glumly, "although I don't feel one hundred percent good about it."

CHAPTER TWENTY THREE

Olivia was relieved when Wayne left to go back to Key West. She needed the time alone to clear her mind and collect her thoughts. It was actually imperative that they be able to go in different directions in order for their partnership to last, she realized. They couldn't agree on everything, nor should they. That was the benefit of having a partner, to be able to see a situation from different points of view. Exploring all kinds of options.

After Wayne was gone, Olivia booked the next flight down to Key Largo. She didn't tell either Alice or Clay she was on her way. It was wonderful to arrive unexpectedly, not giving anyone a chance to prepare. When people were caught unaware, they were often rattled. Then their defenses came down and all kinds of information started spilling out.

Olivia got to the airport early. The day was perfect and the flying conditions unobstructed. In a very short time she would arrive in Key Largo and go straight to Alice and Clay's home. If they weren't there, she'd wait at a nearby hotel until they returned. Somehow, Olivia felt that they were home, though, and that the meeting would be life-changing.

The flight was easy and uneventful, and just as Olivia predicted, in no time at all she found herself getting out of the cab at Alice and Clay's home. As Olivia started to walk down the hill toward the front door a figure suddenly came outside and stood in the shadows under a big tree. Olivia strained to make out who it was, but couldn't be sure. Was the person hiding?

Olivia approached carefully and as she got closer, Alice stepped out onto the path.

"What are you doing here?" Alice's eyes flashed at Olivia. She was dressed in a long khaki dress that didn't fit well. Olivia had never seen her looking so disarrayed.

"I'm just here for a few minutes," Olivia replied.

"A few minutes? Who do you think you're kidding?" Alice was definitely not buying it.

"My visit will be short, Alice," Olivia promised.

"Short or long, who said you're welcome?" Alice stared at Olivia. "You're here to see my husband, aren't you? Okay, let's have it. What do you want with him?"

Olivia was taken aback. "I came to see both of you," she said softly.

"Both of us?" Alice sneered. "So why are you slipping into the house the back way, if you came to see me too? Right now you're headed to Clay's workspace. Why didn't you come around the other side to where both of us live?"

Olivia was jarred. "I didn't realize this wasn't the main entrance," she said.

"Of course you did!" Alice rubbed her foot on the ground. "You came here before with that other detective, didn't you? You know this was where Clay had his studio. And now you're creeping up on him like a thief."

Olivia felt unnerved by Alice's comment.

"You want to steal Clay away from me, too, don't you?" Alice had no intention of allowing Olivia to take a step further. "Well, get in line, honey, there are plenty of others before you who want Clay for their own."

Olivia was electrified. "Who else is trying to steal Clay away from you?" she asked. "Megan?"

Alice laughed. "Sure, Megan tried her best, for starters. And I've recently found out that there's others, too."

Despite her frantic manner, Olivia felt bad for Alice. She remembered that Clay had mentioned that Alice was paranoid, but whether or not that was true, it had to be awful to feel that your husband and marriage were slipping out of your hands. Olivia had been through that with Todd. She realized she had to take charge of the situation quickly. It would calm Alice down if she did.

"Alice, I'm not here to take Clay away," Olivia said swiftly. "That's not my MO. I don't steal other women's men from them. I know how much that hurts. I've been there myself."

That stopped Alice cold. "It's happened to you, too?" she asked, suddenly quieter.

"Yes, it has," Olivia replied.

"Why should I believe you?" Alice was upset.

"Why don't we go to your side of the house now and talk about it more?" asked Olivia. She felt more in command now and Alice sensed it fully.

"Sure, let's go," said Alice. "I need to find out why you really came anyway. Besides, there's plenty I have to tell you, too."

Olivia was pleased by her reaction. "Okay, lead the way," she said, "and I'll follow."

Alice turned and quickly led Olivia along a path that ambled beside a cluster of trees, bushes, and huge wildflowers. They walked for a while until they got to the other side of the property.

"This is the way you enter our joint quarters," Alice announced as they came to a large oak door.

Alice opened the door and they walked into a beautiful, large entrance way with a spiral staircase at the end of it leading to the second floor.

"My personal quarters are upstairs." Alice motioned toward the staircase. "The master bedroom that Clay and I share is down here. Follow me upstairs and we'll have privacy. Clay won't have the least idea that you're here."

Olivia followed Alice up the spiral staircase without another word. "Is Clay in his studio now?" she asked as they both climbed to the second floor.

Alice spun around swiftly. "Why are you asking that? I thought you said you didn't care!"

"I don't," Olivia shot back, realizing how edgy and suspicious Alice was. Clay was right, she definitely seemed to be living on the edge of paranoia, in a hell of her own.

"You do care about Clay, though, don't you?" Alice grew anxious again.

"Alice, you just said Clay wouldn't know I was here. I wondered if he was there, that's all."

"How can I believe you?" asked Alice, looking frantic again as they arrived on the landing of the second floor.

"This place is amazing, it's beautiful," Olivia said, looking around, immediately changing the topic. The hallway had huge glass windows and led to a large, outdoor patio, overlooking willowy trees and a pond.

"Let's go out on the patio and sit under the trees," Alice said as she pushed open the door and they both stepped outside.

Out there it was a wonderland, filled with soft light, the shade of trees, wonderful smells of flowers, and the sound of a pond rippling below.

"Sit down," said Alice, pointing to a comfortable chair.

Olivia sat down, grateful to be out here.

Alice promptly sat beside her. "Okay, what are you really here for, anyway?" she asked. "I heard the case is over and Megan's been arrested. But there's something more, isn't there?"

"There is." Olivia tried to sound conspiratorial.

"Tell me what it is. No one can hear us out here," Alice replied.

"Are we hiding up here?" Olivia asked quickly.

"Not hiding." Alice smirked. "We're just safe and secure. When I want to hide, believe me, I know how!"

"Really?" Olivia was taken aback. "Like how?" She urged Alice onward.

Alice took Olivia right up on it "Remember the time you went looking through Tyron's house for the person peeking in the door?" She suddenly laughed.

"Yes," Olivia murmured, fascinated.

"Well, it was me!" Alice exclaimed proudly, enjoying Olivia's amazement. "That used to be my house too and I had a right to see what was going on! So, from time to time, I'd come and peek through the doors and disappear quickly. I knew how to get out and totally hide."

Olivia shuddered, completely startled to discover it had been Alice peering through the door. What else was there to discover about her?

"No one found out you did that, ever?" asked Olivia intently.

"Never! And I had a right to do it! Don't you think so?" Alice demanded.

Obviously Alice was testing Olivia's loyalty. "You have a right to know what's important." Olivia stayed neutral.

Pleased by Olivia's answer, Alice went on. "Who sent you here to see me, if you didn't come here to be with Clay?"

"I came on my own," Olivia started. "Something in the case still doesn't feel right to me."

"And you don't know what! Am I correct?" Alice looked closely at Olivia.

"Yes, exactly," replied Olivia.

"You guys are working for Megan, aren't you?" Alice rubbed her hand over her face then.

"Yes, we are," said Olivia.

"Why are you still on the case then? I heard it's over now, isn't it?" Alice looked uneasy.

"No, it's not over, that's just a rumor," said Olivia, wanting to unnerve Alice.

"What do you mean it's just rumor?" Alice took the bait.

"New scathing evidence has turned up," Olivia lied, stirring the pot further, wanting to see how Alice would respond.

Alice looked totally alarmed. "What?"

"I'm not at liberty to say exactly." Olivia deliberately played with Alice's mind.

"What do they have? What did they find?" Alice's face began flushing. "What kind of scathing evidence?"

The intensity of Alice's reaction alerted Olivia immediately. What was she so afraid of?

"For starters," Olivia finally declared, "we all definitely need to know more about your marriage to Tyron."

Alice jumped right into the trap. "Me? My marriage? Did that bastard leave papers that revealed something about me? Are you here because of something he implied?"

"Tell me what your marriage to Tyron was really like, Alice." Olivia now dug in forcefully.

Alice started, breathing hard. "From the outside everything looked great. Tyron was wonderful at public displays. Privately, he had his lousy moods, but so does everyone. I put up with it and never said a word. I thought I was happy. Okay? Now tell me what evidence they found!"

Olivia knew she had Alice in the grip of her hand. "First, you tell me more about your marriage," she replied. "Everyone thought you were happy. Was it true? Why wouldn't you be?"

"No reason." Alice breathed raggedly. "After all, I had everything I wanted, didn't I? I had money, daughters, plenty of friends, and I was always in the limelight. But that wasn't the whole picture."

"Did Tyron cheat on you during the marriage?" Olivia wondered if he'd seen escorts then as he did now.

Alice shuddered. "No, not at all! That was one thing I never would have put up with and Tyron knew it, too. Even though he got moody, he didn't want to lose me. I kept his life together in all kinds of ways. And I told him over and over, if ever there was anyone else, I would be gone instantly!"

"Then one night Megan walked into the picture, didn't she?" Olivia upped the ante.

"That's right," Alice snapped. "Okay, I told you a lot. Now tell me, what's the evidence?"

Olivia stayed single-minded. "I can't yet," she insisted. "Keep telling me about your marriage."

Alice closed her eyes suddenly, as though she were growing dizzy. "Why can't you yet?"

"When I tell you finally, you'll understand," breathed Olivia. She knew she had Alice in her grip and had to keep pressing.

"It's awful, isn't it? It's about me?" Alice wailed suddenly.

"Yes, it's about you, Alice." Olivia played along. "Tell me more, right now! It will help you."

"Tyron and I had been married a long time when he met Megan." Alice was growing frantic. "I knew he was getting bored and restless. I knew I no longer held any fascination for him, but I never knew that everything we had together would disappear in a flash. That my whole life would be snuffed out overnight."

Olivia could only imagine how awful that had to have been. But she couldn't sympathize with Alice now, though. In fact, Olivia had to get her more upset. The more upset Alice was, the more she would reveal. Olivia felt close to a full revelation.

"Megan must have been beautiful, too," Olivia commented, intensifying the pain.

"Who the hell cares?" Alice practically spat on the floor. "Megan was rotten and no good and, in the long run, she and Tyron deserved each other. I always knew something bad would happen to both of them. You don't do what they did with no consequences."

"You always knew Tyron would die?" Olivia took a sharp breath.

"Not that exactly," said Alice. "But I knew something awful would happen."

"Like what?" Olivia was alerted.

"For a while I thought just being married to Megan was going to be awful enough for him!" Alice jeered. "I knew she'd end up making a fool of him, like he made a fool of me."

"And she did, didn't she?" Olivia urged Alice on.

"Yes, of course she did," said Alice. "Everybody knew he was seeing those other girls. And believe it or not, I felt badly for Tyron. I kept visiting him and telling him to get rid of Megan like he got rid of me. What did he need her for now? I also told him to get rid of the escorts and take me back again. We could have our old life and become a family again."

"Tyron wasn't into it, though?"

"He laughed at me and said forget about it, honey, what's over is over. Our time together is done."

"That had to be humiliating for you, Alice," said Olivia.

"In a way yes, in a way no," Alice murmured. "For a long time I didn't believe it. I believed Tyron got off on it that I still cared. I could see that he enjoyed my visits, and I kept waiting for him to tell me I was the only one he ever really loved."

"He didn't, though, did he?"

"No, he never did. Finally, one day, I had enough." Alice's face contorted. "I was sick of being made a fool of. You know that moment comes to us all."

"I know." Olivia nodded.

"Enough was enough!" Alice's voice rose. "I suddenly decided to do him one better. I was still pretty enough, and had plenty of his money, to boot."

"So you decided to marry a young guy yourself!" Olivia jumped in.

"Absolutely right." Alice's eyes shot fire. "I'd show the bastard how it felt."

"You married Clay to get back at Tyron?" Olivia breathed.

"Partially, that's true! And also to make myself feel good again." Alice looked briefly triumphant.

"Did it work, Alice?" Olivia began to feel edgy.

"For a while it did," Alice breathed. "Believe it or not, for a while Clay and I were happy. Until the bitch came back onto the scene again!"

"Megan?"

"The bitch! The bitch!" Alice yelled. "All of a sudden, out of the blue, Megan started throwing herself at Clay, right in front of my eyes."

"How did Clay handle it?" Olivia was spellbound.

"He said he didn't give a damn, but he lied. I could see that he went for her hook, line, and sinker," Alice cried out. "And people at the club we went to saw it too. Hank even warned me."

"Who's Hank?" Olivia was spellbound.

"Hank's my friend at the club. He used to be Clay's friend, but now he's mine, too. Hank cares about me, wants what's right for me." Alice was sputtering. "He told me it wasn't enough that Megan took Tyron, now she's after your second husband, too!"

"Horrible, really horrible," Olivia couldn't help but cry out.

"More than horrible." Alice jumped up out of her chair and then sat down again quickly.

"When did you find out that Clay and Megan were actually seeing each other?" Olivia needed details.

Alice shook her head wildly back and forth. "The first time I asked Clay if he was involved with Megan, he swore to me that they were just friends. He got down on his knees and swore that he wasn't sleeping with her. For a little while I believed him, but then I kept wondering. When I brought it up over and over Clay would say I was paranoid. I really found out, though, when Hank got me the receipt and photos from the hotel in Mexico."

"What was Hank doing there with them?" Olivia immediately felt odd about it. What was his part in this? What was he getting out of it?

"Hank went down there with Clay for a few days," Alice continued. "They were both setting up an art exhibit. But I had no idea at all Megan would be there. Neither did Tyron, or anyone else."

"Is Hank an artist too?" asked Olivia. "Is he successful like Clay?"

"He will be successful one day if I have anything to say about it," Alice breathed, her eyes darting back and forth wildly.

Olivia's heart started beating fast. "So then Hank took the picture of Clay and Megan there and betrayed his friend?"

"Hank didn't betray anybody." Alice gasped. "He was looking after me, and doing what was right. After I got the photo I also did what was right! I took it over to Tyron and let him see it for himself. Then I begged him to write Megan out of his will. The bastard said no, again. Whatever I wanted, he refused. He did it later, but to me he said no. Something snapped then. Megan couldn't have both my husbands. I couldn't let her have both Tyron and Clay." Alice's eyes looked half crazed now.

"You couldn't let her do that, so what did you do?" Olivia felt her heart sinking.

"I did what I had to," Alice suddenly wailed. "You would do it, too. Any woman would!"

A shock of silence descended upon them then as Alice's words hung in the air. Suddenly the clouds in Olivia's mind parted and she saw what had happened clearly.

"So you took Tyron from Megan then, didn't you?" Olivia exclaimed.

Alice smiled oddly. "I did," she whispered, seemingly victorious. "I knew Hank would help me too, and he did. I arranged for him to be there on the patio when Tyron was alone. The night before he pushed him, we placed a huge rock at the foot of the stairs. Then the next day, Hank crawled up onto the deck from behind and then wheeled Tyron's wheelchair to the top of the stairs. After that all it took was one push. The rest is history."

"You had Tyron killed!" Olivia could barely breathe.

"I had no choice, I had to." Alice started to moan. "And I did everything in my power to make it look like Megan's fault."

"What did Hank get out of it? Money?" Olivia was beside herself.

"He got plenty of money, but so what?" Alice began sobbing uncontrollably.

Olivia's heart was beating wildly. Thank God she had a recorder on under her dress. "Tell me more, Alice, more!"

"I heard that Tyron finally wrote Megan out of his will a few days before he died." Alice was wailing now. "It was too late, though. Too late for everything! All this time and he refused to ever take me back!"

Olivia froze completely. Despite her wild, desperate manner, Alice knew exactly what she was doing.

"So now you know what happened, but you can't do anything to me." Alice stared at Olivia boldly. "And why should you? I'm not to blame. It's not my fault! It's Megan who deserves to be locked up forever."

"It is your fault," Olivia whispered, in a grating tone.

Alice blanched. "I thought you said you understood. I thought you said the same thing happened to you. I thought we were sisters."

"I never had someone thrown down the stairs," Olivia retorted sharply. "And you're trying to put an innocent woman away!"

"Megan is not innocent! She ruins one life after another!" Alice turned pale suddenly.

"And what about Tyron?" Olivia exclaimed.

"Tyron deserved it." Alice looked at Olivia with pleading eyes. "He tortured so many people."

"Alice, I have to bring you back up to Naples with me and to the police station," Olivia said.

"You're crazy, you're nasty," Alice spit back.

"I have no choice about it," said Olivia.

"You set me up, you tried to trick me!" Alice jumped up then and rushed over to the patio railing, crouching beside it and holding on tight. "Another betrayal! I can't take any more."

Olivia leapt out of her chair and followed her there. "Don't be afraid, please," said Olivia. "I didn't betray you, I'm doing what's right. I'll make sure they treat you fairly. You're not well. You're in great mental distress."

Alice became livid. "I'm not in mental distress! I did what I had to and I'm not sorry!"

"I have to call the police station down here then to come and arrest you," said Olivia firmly.

"They'll never believe you." Alice grew pale. "I'll deny I ever said a word to you."

"I have a recorder on me," Olivia told her. "Every word you've said has been recorded. Please come with me calmly instead."

"A recorder?" Alice's eyes opened wide, filled with bewilderment and fury. "You recorded everything I said?"

"I had to, it's for your own good too." Olivia began shouting. "You're sick, you need help."

"Not me! Never!" Alice howled and in a moment of horror, she quickly straightened up, leapt into the air, and hurled herself onto the railing.

"Alice, stop, stop," Olivia yelled as Alice, in the flash of a second, plunged headfirst onto the pavement below.

"Alice! Alice!" Olivia began screaming, as she looked down at the lifeless body, sprawled out motionlessly.

CHAPTER TWENTY FOUR

Olivia ran downstairs in a daze and huddled under the tree beside Alice. But her body was totally numb now, no pulse, no breath, no sign of life. Olivia quickly swooped down over the body to resuscitate it, but whatever she did, there was no response. Was this real? How could it be happening? Olivia felt as though she were caught in a horrible dream.

Exhausted and shaking from head to toe, Olivia quickly grabbed her phone to put in a call for help. She called 911 and reported what had gone on. Help was on the way immediately, they assured her.

Then Olivia quickly put a call in to Wayne. Thankfully, he picked right up.

"Alice jumped off her balcony!" Olivia's heart was pounding and she could barely get the words out. "She dead here, sprawled on the ground."

"What? What?" Wayne was dumbfounded.

"We were talking, I pressed her, challenged her, and she confessed to having Tyron killed." Olivia's words spilled out over one another uncontrollably. "I have it all on recording."

"Stay where you are. Don't move, please." Wayne went into high gear. "I'll be there as soon as I possibly can."

After she hung up Olivia sat under the tree, frozen. The police would arrive in a few minutes, but where was Clay? Was he at home in his studio? Somehow Olivia didn't think so. She also didn't think she could face him, or anyone, now. Was this her fault? Olivia had known Alice was crazy, but had no idea she was this close to the edge. Had Olivia pushed her too far? Olivia sat there huddled under the tree.

Before long local police officers arrived and swarmed through the property.

"Officer Tauber here," a tall heavyset gentleman introduced himself to Olivia. "I understand you're a detective here on a case?"

"I pushed her too far." Olivia voice broke as she answered. "The dead woman confessed to having her ex-husband killed. I have it all here on recording."

"Good," Tauber exclaimed. "Let me listen to the recording, and I'll give it right back."

Olivia handed him the recording, her hands shaking.

"I offered to take her to the police station myself." Olivia felt herself babbling. "She wouldn't go. When I finally said I'd have to call you to come and arrest her, she suddenly swung herself down over the railing."

"Come on inside with me," said Tauber. "I'll get you a glass of water."

"I can't." Olivia started to cry. "Let me stay here with her for a little while."

"It's not a good idea," he said.

"Please, please," Olivia wept.

"For a little while," Tauber said quietly, "but then you have to go inside. I have to help the other officers now and we also have to contact the family."

Olivia couldn't even begin to imagine the pain they would all be in. She also couldn't help but think of the way Alice's death resembled Tyron's. Like him, she fell from a height to the ground.

Officer Tauber left to join the other officers and make the calls. As Olivia sat alone, wave upon wave of horror engulfed her. She watched some of the officers tie yellow tape around the trees and others take photographs of the body from every angle. Then, as the sun slowly faded through the trees, they finally covered Alice up completely.

Although part of her felt responsible, Olivia also struggled to realize that she was not fully to blame. Perhaps this sudden death was easier for Alice than a life locked up in jail? Olivia also wondered where Clay had been when it happened and how he would react when he heard the news. Would he be relieved? Alice's relationship with Clay was also part of what pushed her. So many factors had led to this horrible act.

Another officer, Ben, then approached Olivia gingerly. "Why don't you come inside and have something to drink?" he now asked. "It's not good to sit out here alone."

"My partner is coming from Naples soon," Olivia breathed.

Ben nodded. "But he's not here now, come on inside."

"Is Clay there?" asked Olivia, frightened to see him.

"No, he wasn't at the home when his wife jumped," Ben responded.

Olivia still couldn't move. "I'll come inside a little later," she said.

"Whatever you like," said Ben as he leaned toward her then. "Look, I know this had to be shocking for you. It's not your fault, though. You have to realize that."

Olivia looked up at him, grateful. "Thank you," she said. "I do."

"These things happen all the time," Ben went on. "It's part of the job. You can't take it personally."

"Thanks again," Olivia replied, as Ben stood up and took a few steps away. "I'll go inside in a little while."

After Ben left, Olivia went to the other side of the tree and sat with her head in her hands. Olivia knew she wasn't responsible for Alice's choices, but how was it possible not to be swamped by the pain? Olivia also knew that when someone took their own life, they always brought down others who had been close to them. The memory of it could haunt that person's entire life. Olivia couldn't let that happen and she wouldn't.

As the day started to fade, Olivia looked up finally and saw someone approaching from the distance.

"Olivia, Olivia," the voice was calling to her. For a second Olivia didn't recognize the voice. "I'm here, Olivia. Where are you?"

Then, through the haze of pain she was feeling, Olivia suddenly recognized Wayne. She stood up quickly under the tree and waved as he approached in the distance.

"Olivia!" Wayne ran over to her. "Thank God, you're all right! Thank God, she didn't throw you over the railing with her."

Then, in a swift, shocking moment, Wayne pulled Olivia to him in a fervent embrace. Before Olivia knew what was happening, her lips met Wayne's and they suddenly started kissing passionately.

It was a stunning kiss, entirely unexpected and life-giving in every way. Olivia and Wayne held each other tightly. When Olivia finally came back to herself, there she was, nestled in the warmth and strength of Wayne's arms.

When Olivia and Wayne drew apart they stared at each other, both utterly shocked. This was the last thing either of them planned for. But the intensity of the moment took over and had its say.

"I'm so sorry I wasn't here with you when this happened," Wayne breathed then. "How awful to have to go through something like this alone."

"I wasn't alone," Olivia breathed softly then. "You came in a few minutes. And I knew that you would."

"Come inside now, please." Wayne kept his arms around her. "This has been an awful shock. It will take time to come back to yourself."

There had been many shocks that afternoon, thought Olivia, not the least of which was the way her relationship with Wayne had now completely turned around.

*

Before long, reporters began to flood into Alice's home and the story was blasted all over the news. Tyron's murder was finally solved. Olivia Wells, private detective, once again had found the true culprit. Megan, Tyron's widow, was innocent, and would be let out of custody in a short while.

Olivia took no joy in her personal acclaim. Everyone had worked hard on the case. She had just insisted upon going on the last leg of the journey, when others thought it was done. Olivia was relieved, though, about Megan. Whether or not people liked Megan or the way she lived, she was innocent of Tyron's death. And Olivia and Wayne had done the job Megan hired them to do and cleared her name.

Officer Tauber came over to Olivia and Wayne shortly after the news broke.

"Clay was located in Naples, at the prison, visiting Megan," Tauber reported. "He said he told Alice that morning he was going to visit her there. Alice begged him not to. Clay said he told Alice he had no choice about it. He couldn't leave Megan there alone."

Olivia felt better hearing that. She realized even more fully then that Alice had jumped to get away from many things, including her dissolving relationship with Clay. Although Olivia was a witness to it, she wasn't to blame.

"How is Clay handling Alice's death?" asked Olivia.

"He's calm about it," Tauber replied. "He said that Alice had been threatening suicide for a long time now if Clay didn't stay away from Megan."

Olivia flinched. She knew how important it was to pay attention to threats of those kinds. Clay was aware of how Alice felt and visited Megan anyway.

"Does Clay have some responsibility for what happened to Alice?" Olivia asked.

"We can't go there, it's beyond our scope," Tauber cut her off quickly. "Clay wasn't there, he didn't push her. But from what I've heard, Alice did arrange to have Hank push Tyron to his death. The police in Naples are taking Hank in as we speak."

"It's interesting that Alice died the same way that Tyron did," Wayne remarked.

"Yes, but no one pushed her," Tauber interjected. "She did it to herself."

"Her destiny pushed her," Wayne said in an odd tone.

"Well, I don't know about something like that," said Tauber.

"Where is Clay now?" Wayne was curious.

"He's on his way back down here to make funeral arrangements," Tauber replied. "Alice's daughters, Kayle and Lana, are also on their way down. Both of them refuse to speak to anyone. They're totally inconsolable."

"I'm sorry to hear that," said Olivia.

"Well, anyway, you did a fantastic job," Tauber repeated. "Feel happy about that."

Olivia looked at Wayne somberly. "How can we feel happy that the case is solved when there's sorrow here everywhere you look?" she murmured.

"Solving cases is bittersweet," Wayne replied quietly. "Some benefit, others suffer a lot."

That was a good way to put it, thought Olivia. And, strangely enough, she and Wayne had been the ones who had benefited. They'd turned a corner together. Their relationship was now completely new.

"There are many reporters who want to speak to you guys," Tauber said. "I also heard that calls are pouring in for you both with new cases."

Wayne shook his head slowly. "Don't we get a little special time to be alone together first?" he asked Olivia, his eyes suddenly twinkling.

Olivia smiled.

"Let's see who's calling first," she replied.

About Jaden Skye

#1 bestselling author Jaden Skye is author of the bestselling romantic suspense series CARIBBEAN MURDER, which includes 16 books (and counting), and which begins with DEATH BY HONEYMOON (Book #1).

Jaden is also author of the romance series A PERFECT STRANGER.

Jaden is also author of the new romantic suspense series MURDER IN THE KEYS, which begins with NO PLACE TO DIE (Book #1).

Jaden has always been fascinated with mystery, wrongful death, lies, deception and the power of the truth to prevail. Her romantic suspense/mystery novels feature strong female protagonists who must overcome insurmountable obstacles, and through them, she seeks to get to the very heart of the nature of justice and love. Please visit www.jadenskye.com to find links to stay in touch with Jaden via Facebook, Twitter, Goodreads, her blog, and a whole bunch of other places. Jaden loves to hear from you, so don't be shy and check back often!

Books by Jaden Skye

THE CARIBBEAN MURDER SERIES
DEATH BY HONEYMOON (Book #1)
DEATH BY DIVORCE (Book #2)
DEATH BY MARRIAGE (Book #3)
DEATH BY DESIRE (Book #4)
DEATH BY DECEIT (Book #5)
DEATH BY JEALOUSY (Book #6)
DEATH BY PROPOSAL (Book #7)
DEATH BY OBSESSION (Book #8)
DEATH BY DEVOTION (Book #9)
DEATH BY BETRAYAL (Book #10)
DEATH BY REQUEST (Book #11)
DEATH BY ENGAGEMENT (Book #12)
DEATH BY SEDUCTION (Book #13)
DEATH BY TEMPTATION (Book #14)
DEATH BY INVITATION (Book #15)
DEATH BY WEDDING (Book #16)

THE TOM'S RIVER SAGA
A PERFECT STRANGER (Book #1)

MURDER IN THE KEYS
NO PLACE TO DIE (Book #1)
NO PLACE TO VANISH (Book #2)
NO PLACE FOR VENGEANCE (Book #3)
NO PLACE FOR MARRIAGE (Book #4)

THE KILLING GAME
INVITATION TO DIE (Book #1)
INVITATION TO MADNESS (Book #2)
INVITATION TO AGONY (Book #3)

Made in the USA
Middletown, DE
16 March 2020

86484380R00096